BREAKING DAWN

DELTA FORCE STRONG BOOK #8

ELLE JAMES

TWISTED PAGE INC

BREAKING DAWN

DELTA FORCE STRONG BOOK #8

New York Times & USA Today
Bestselling Author

ELLE JAMES

Copyright © 2021 by Elle James

All rights reserved.

No part of this book may be reproduced in any form or by any electronic or mechanical means, including information storage and retrieval systems, without written permission from the author, except for the use of brief quotations in a book review.

EBOOK ISBN: 978-1-62695-381-9

PRINT ISBN: 978-1-62695-683-4

Dedicated to my pups who keep me moving when I would sit all day. Getting up fifty times an hour to take them outside makes me limber, nimble and less sedentary. Love my Bandit and Charli.
Elle James

AUTHOR'S NOTE

Enjoy other military books by Elle James

Delta Force Strong
Ivy's Delta (Delta Force 3 Crossover)
Breaking Silence (#1)
Breaking Rules (#2)
Breaking Away (#3)
Breaking Free (#4)
Breaking Hearts (#5)
Breaking Ties (#6)
Breaking Point (#7)
Breaking Dawn (#8)
Breaking Promises (#9)

Visit ellejames.com for titles and release dates
For hot cowboys, visit her alter ego Myla Jackson at
mylajackson.com
and join Elle James's Newsletter at
https://ellejames.com/contact/

CHAPTER 1

SERGEANT FIRST CLASS Lance Rankin strode toward the two Black Hawk helicopters, rotors turning, on the tarmac at an Israeli airbase near Jerusalem. Having just arrived in the country to augment a special mission, he hefted the bag containing his submachine gun and ammo. He leaned close to his Delta Force counterpart, who'd been in the country longer than him, to receive the briefing he'd hoped to have *before* they moved out.

"Glad you made it," Master Sergeant Ketchum yelled over the noise of the engines. "We'll have to brief you on the way. Intel indicated that our target will be moved to an undisclosed location tomorrow. It's now or never if we want to get him out."

"Give me the details," Lance said.

Ketchum nodded and continued toward the aircraft. "You'll be working directly with Mika Blue of the Israeli Defense Force, who's part of the point team. Once the team breaches the building, you and Blue will grab the target and get him to the extraction point. Blue is a skilled fighter and can interpret."

"Who is our target?" Lance asked.

"I'll brief you once we're all on board. For now, meet the Deltas. I'm going to check on the other members of our combined team." Ketchum turned and hurried back the way they'd come.

Lance climbed into the Black Hawk and settled on the bench beside another Delta Force operative balancing a sniper rifle between his knees. He wore a black armored vest loaded with numerous magazines and a couple of hand grenades. He gave Lance a chin lift and held out his hand. "Gonzo."

Lance shook his hand. "Lance Rankin."

Gonzo frowned. "Call sign?"

Lance shrugged. "Lance."

"No nickname?" The man's eyes narrowed as he studied Lance, his gaze taking in the scar next to Lance's left eye. "We'll have to fix that. How about Scar, Phantom or Freddy?"

Lance's lips twisted. "Or Lance or Rankin."

Gonzo shook his head. "What do you like to do when you're not out playing Army?"

Again, he shrugged. "I like to hike, run and build computers."

"How about Hiker or Runner?" Gonzo suggested.

"Or Hack..." the guy across from his said.

"Hack, it is," Gonzo grinned. "Welcome to the team, Hack."

Though he was "on loan," Lance would be a part of this unique team organized to perform a dangerous extraction. That had been all the information he'd been given before he'd left Fort Hood less than twenty-four hours ago. He'd been assured he'd be briefed once he had boots on the ground in Israel.

The man seated on the other side of Gonzo leaned forward, hand outstretched. "Bass."

Lance shook his hand and the hands of the other two Deltas seated across from him.

"Smoke," the one who'd suggested Hack was the smaller guy of the two, wiry and rugged.

Gonzo tipped his chin toward him. "He likes to pop smoke whenever he can. Likes a dramatic entrance."

The guy beside him was tall and lean. "Ice."

"On account of he doesn't get flustered when shit hits the fan," Smoke said.

"He keeps so cool, you'd get frostbite if you touched him," Gonzo added.

"Whatever," Ice said. "They tell you anything about this mission?"

"Not yet."

Ice snorted. "Gonna be a shit show."

Lance didn't like the sound of that. "How so?"

Smoke jabbed Ice with his elbow. "Let Ketchum give him the low down."

"Yeah," Gonzo said. "Let Ketchum." He nodded toward the man headed their way. "Here comes the rest of the team."

Ice snorted again. "Good thing the other Hawk is filled with more Deltas."

"How did we get stuck in this one?" Ice asked.

Gonzo grinned. "Hand selected for our skills, no doubt."

As the soldiers neared the helicopter, Lance's brow furrowed. One was shorter than Ketchum and appeared to be a lightweight, seeming too small to carry a rifle, ammo and wear an armored vest. "Are we teaming with a kid?" Lance asked.

"Worse," Ice said through gritted teeth.

"Woman," Smoke said, his tone flat, his lips pressing into a thin line.

"Hey." Gonzo glared at them. "Those soldiers, male and female, have as much or more combat time than either one of you. They're highly decorated in the Israeli Defense Force and members of the Sayeret Matkal—the equivalent of our Delta Force. So, don't judge one of them based on her gender. She earned her rank."

Ketchum and the five members of the IDF climbed on board. Ketchum directed the woman to take the seat beside Lance. Sliding onto the bench across from her, the Master Sergeant leaned forward. "Lance Rankin—"

"It's Hack," Gonzo interrupted. "For the purpose of this mission, he'll be Hack."

Ketchum nodded. "Hack…" He tipped his head toward the woman. "Meet Mikayla Blum."

She held out her hand, her lips twisting. "For the purpose of this mission, call me Mika Blue. Nice to meet you." Her voice was firm and her English perfect, with no hint of an accent. American English.

He took her small hand in his, surprised at the strength of her grip, despite her soft skin. All the while, he shook her hand, he couldn't help thinking, *Holy shit, we're going into enemy territory with a female.* Some men viewed females on the battlefield as bad luck. Two members of the team he'd be working with had already voiced their displeasure.

Now, Lance understood why he'd been hand-picked for this mission.

Mika lifted her chin and met his gaze head-on. "I understand you fought against ISIS alongside an all-female Kurdish militia."

He nodded. "I did. They were some of the bravest and most fierce fighters I've had the honor of serving with."

Ice cursed.

Smoke muttered, "You could have said something."

Lance ignored them and focused on the woman who'd take point with him. "Been a member of Sayeret Matkal long?" he asked.

She nodded. "Long enough. Over four years." Her gaze left his as she checked her gear. A moment later, she looked up and pinned him with her brown-black gaze. "Have you been a member of Delta Force for long?"

He fought a grin. "Eight years and some change." He liked that she wasn't backing down or letting him off lightly. As a female fighter in an elite force in a part of the world where men believed a woman's place was in the home, she had to have dealt with a great deal of flak from her male counterparts.

Fortunately, his experience with the female militia had changed his attitude about women in combat. He'd still felt protective of them, but no more so than other members of his team. Well, maybe a little more protective. Some of them had left children at home with grandparents while fighting to drive ISIS from their country. Still, he'd never been on an extraction mission with women as part of his team.

Ketchum leaned toward Lance. "We've been tasked to rescue and return Deputy Defense Minister Efraim Yaron. Hamas captured him while he was on a diplomatic visit to Lebanon."

Ketchum pulled out a computer tablet, tapped the screen with his finger and brought up a satellite image. "He's being held in the ruins of a bombed-out Palestinian village. Intel in the sky and on the ground indicates he's in the only building that remained intact. Here." He pointed at the screen where a white square of a building stood on the edge of the crumbled bricks and shells of those less fortunate structures.

"We'll land on the other side of this ridge from the village and go in on foot. Once we have Yaron, the choppers will meet us here." He pointed to a clearing not far from the building. "We anticipate twenty-five to thirty Hamas soldiers in attendance. Our team of twenty will move in, subdue the guards, clear the building and retrieve Yaron." He glanced up. "Questions?"

"Are they equipped with anti-aircraft weapons?" Lance asked.

"They have access to rocket-propelled grenades they've used in the past to target Israeli gunships. Whether they have them in the village, we don't know."

Lance nodded. "So, we assume yes, for planning purposes." He reached for the tablet and studied the terrain leading from the ridge to the structure where Hamas allegedly held Yaron. He frowned and pointed at a rock bluff behind the building. "Is that a drop-off?"

Ketchum nodded. "Intel on the ground estimates it's a two-hundred-foot cliff. Bravo Team, that's us, will get into position along the ridge and wait until Alpha Team circles around that cliff and establishes a perimeter surrounding the village. They will move in to tighten the perimeter to make certain no one alerts Hamas or enters the village while we're conducting our extraction. Once they're in place, we'll rappel in, take out the guards, clear the building and extract the diplomat."

Lance zoomed in on the terrain. The two-dimensional image did little to indicate how steep the hill was on either side of the cliff or any potential drop-offs that might be hidden from the satellite cameras by trees or other vegetation. Lance liked it better when they practiced maneuvers before executing them. With Hamas scheduled to move Yaron the next day, they didn't have time for such luxuries.

He turned to Mika. "Have you ever rappelled?"

She nodded. "I have. I've trained others as well."

"We have everything we'll need to get to the bottom of that cliff. It's the fastest, quietest way in. We'll take out any rear guards using rifles with silencers." Ketchum nodded toward Gonzo. "Gonzo is one of our best snipers. He'll cover us from the ridgeline."

The team performed a communications check while in route, ensuring all radios were functioning and on the same frequency. The IDF fighters had all been equipped with radio headsets similar to those used by the Deltas.

Lance checked and double-checked his rifle, pistol, gear and ammo. In his peripheral vision, he noted Mika doing the same. Once she was finished, she sat staring out the side door of the Black Hawk, her rifle resting across her knees, pointing out the door.

A dozen questions simmered in Lance's mind as he studied the woman who would be his partner, storming the building and freeing the Israeli diplomat. Chit-chat was held to a minimum, with the noise of the helicopter engines and rotors roaring in their ears. At the same time, the aircraft ate the distance between the airbase and their landing zone deep in Palestinian territory.

What felt like hours later, the helicopters slowed and lowered.

Lance's pulse quickened, and adrenaline surged through his system.

Game time.

CHAPTER 2

As soon as the helicopter touched the ground in a valley west of the village, Alpha and Bravo teams leaped out. The helicopters lifted into the air and flew a safe distance away.

The twenty-man team navigated the terrain, ascending the hill. Once they reached the top, Alpha Team immediately split and circled the cliff, finding their way down the other side on a gentler slope.

Bravo team set up the rappelling gear, anchoring four ropes securely around trees or boulders and leaving their lengths coiled at the top of the cliff, ready to lower them when they received word from Alpha Team that the village perimeter had been secured. The members of Bravo Team tied six-foot lengths of rope around their legs and waists to form seats and clipped a D-ring to the harness in front.

Once they were ready, Bravo Team crept to the

edge of the ridgeline. Gonzo had already established his position and surveyed the village below through his scope and night-vision goggles.

Lance settled on the ground beside Mika's slim form decked out in combat gear, her hair pulled into a single ponytail, hanging halfway down her back.

"Have you always wanted to be in the military?" he asked, his voice barely above a whisper.

She gave him a brief glance, cocking an eyebrow. "Have you?"

He nodded and studied the buildings and terrain below. "My mother and father were both in the Army. My grandfather was a Marine. It was in my blood."

Mika nodded. "My mother died when I was six. My father was in the Army. He did the best he could with a daughter."

"He did a good job," Lance said. "From what I understand, it's difficult to complete the training to get into Sayeret Matkal. The fact that you did it is impressive."

She shot another glance in his direction, the starlight shining down on her narrowed eyes. "Meaning a woman is less likely than a man to complete the training successfully?"

"Not at all. Anyone completing the training is impressive." Lance grinned and changed the subject. "If you were a brat like me, you must have grown up near a military installation."

"I did." Mika's gaze returned to the village again. "They brought you all the way from Fort Hood, Texas, just for this mission." It was a statement, not a question.

Lance grinned. "Were they afraid no one else could get along with you?"

Mika's body stiffened. "I asked for someone who'd fought alongside women. I didn't want someone who felt like he had to protect me when, in fact, I might be the one to protect him. We have a mission to perform, a life to save. We cannot afford distractions based on gender."

Lance gave her a mock salute. "Message received, loud and clear."

Her shoulders relaxed a little. "Did they pull you from another mission to come here?"

Lance shook his head. "No. I was scheduled for some R&R."

She looked his way, her brow furrowing. "R&R?"

"Vacation." He found himself studying her face in the starlight. She had high cheekbones and a strong jawline, but her lips were full and soft. When she wasn't frowning, her brows winged upward, as dark as her ponytail and surprisingly delicate. She was a striking woman.

"Where were you going on vacation?" she asked.

"I was going to rent a cabin close to the fort on Belton Lake and do a little boating and fishing. My buddies were going to join me on the weekend. It's something different than hanging out at the Salty Dog, our usual haunt." He'd asked Rucker Sloan, his teammate, to take over his cabin and boat rental reservation. The team would have been disappointed if he'd canceled. They had all planned on crashing his vacation when they got off duty that weekend. Blade and his girl, Sophia, had volunteered to bring the booze. Dash was bringing the music. Rucker and Tank had volunteered to supply the steaks. Everyone was bringing something. As much time as they spent together on missions and during the workweek, it was always fun to get together out of uniform and away from the structured environment of the military.

"You didn't have to come," she said. "Surely, they could have found someone else."

He shrugged. "Maybe they asked around, and I was the only one available. It doesn't matter. I'm here now."

"My father used to take me fishing when he was off duty," she said quietly.

"Is he still in the military?" Lance asked.

She shook her head. "He retired several years ago. Now, he consults with them on a part-time basis and goes fishing whenever he can." A smile curled her lips, transforming her face from the tough soldier to a softer version of herself.

Lance fought to tear his gaze away from her and

focus on the village below. "You and your father are close?"

She nodded. "After my mother died, it was just the two of us muddling through life together."

"He never remarried?"

"No." She sighed. "He loved my mother so much. It broke his heart when she died."

"I'm sorry for your loss, and his," Lance said softly.

Her grip shifted on her rifle. "It was a long time ago. I barely remember her." She tipped her head toward him. "She was American. She insisted that I claim dual citizenship when I was born. And in her honor, my father sent me to college in the States."

"That's why you speak English with an American accent. Where did you go to college?"

That smile was back, making Lance's heart skip several beats. "I attended the University of Texas in Austin."

He chuckled. "That's not far from Fort Hood."

"I know," she said. "I'm familiar with the area and hope to go back for a visit someday. My mother grew up in a little town called Salado. I visited Salado when I was in Texas, but my grandparents had since passed, and the house had been sold to a young couple with children. I didn't bother them. But it was interesting seeing the house where my mother spent her childhood. I liked Salado. It seemed…"

"Peaceful?" he prompted.

"Yeah." She gave a crooked grin. "It's been a long time since I thought about that visit."

"If you two are finished flirting, could you focus on the mission?" Ketchum's voice sounded in Lance's headset.

Lance started to say he hadn't been flirting, thought better of it, and answered, "Roger." He pulled his night-vision goggles in place and studied the rear of the building that backed up against the cliff.

From two hundred feet above, he could just make out a single sentry standing guard at the rear entrance that led out onto what had probably once been a back patio and garden but was now overgrown with weeds and brush.

"Alpha Team is in place." The words were whispered into Lance's headset.

"Let's roll." Ketchum inched to the edge of the cliff and lowered his rope quietly to the bottom. Then he slipped the rope through the D-Ring attached to his seat.

Ice and two Israeli soldiers had also hooked up to the long ropes.

Ketchum nodded toward Gonzo. "Ready?"

Gonzo answered. "Roger."

As one, the four men slipped silently over the edge and dropped out of sight.

Lance crept to the edge and looked over, his gaze following the paths of the men descending to the base of the cliff. He focused his night-vision goggles on the man leaning against the back door of the building, as he was sure Gonzo was doing as well.

The sentry straightened, and his head tipped upward.

"He's spotted them," Lance murmured, his heartbeat quickening.

No sooner had the words left his mouth than a muffled thump sounded behind him.

The man at the back door dropped to his knees and then face-planted in the dirt.

By then, Ketchum, Smoke and the two IDF soldiers were on the ground.

"We're up." Lance slipped the rope through his D-Ring, glanced across at Mika and checked that she'd hooked up correctly. She was already backing over the edge, one hand on the rope in front of her, the other with the rope tucked behind her back. She gave him a chin lift, eased over the edge, and then pushed out and away from the rocky face of the cliff, letting the rope slide through her gloved hands. In several bounds, she was at the bottom.

Lance followed close behind, gliding down the rope with the ease of experience, much like Mika. She hadn't batted an eyelash over the two-hundred-foot drop, taking it in stride as if she'd done it a thousand times before. And she probably had.

As soon as Ice made it down, the team entered the building through the rear and moved down a dark hallway using their goggles, clearing each room, one at a time, silencers making their movements silent and deadly. Ahead of Lance and Mika, Ketchum and Smoke took out two Hamas soldiers asleep on the floor of one room, their weapons lying beside them. Across the hall, one of the IDF soldiers eliminated another member of Hamas as he opened the door, carrying a rifle slung over his shoulder. The man hit the ground, his rifle clattering loudly.

Ketchum, Ice and Smoke hurried to keep others from emerging from their rooms to see what the commotion was all about. They disappeared around a corner, followed by two of the IDF soldiers.

Mika, Lance and the remaining two Israeli members of Alpha Team hurried to catch up to the others. As Lance neared the corner, someone shouted, and the loud crack of gunfire announced to anyone in the building that they were under attack.

Lance darted his head around the corner.

Ketchum, Ice, Smoke and the Israelis lay flat on their bellies in a large room, firing at another hallway on the opposite side. A rifle barrel poked out, the gunman firing indiscriminately.

Lance spotted a doorway in the larger room, four feet from where he stood. He waited for the gunman to quit firing, bunched his muscles and raced for the door.

At the same time, Mika dashed past him and reached the door before him. She yanked it open, dove through, hit the ground and rolled to her feet, her rifle ready and aimed in front of her. The doorway led to a staircase leading to the second level. Mika took the lead. Lance fought the urge to yank her back and take point. He had to remind himself that she was a combat veteran with their elite special forces. She knew what she was doing.

He followed, covering her six, prepared to provide cover when she needed it.

The loud sound of gunfire below echoed off the walls.

Footsteps pounded ahead, and a shout sounded.

Mika cursed. "They're ordering them to kill the prisoner." She raced up the steps.

Lance took the steps two at a time with his long legs, quickly catching up to Mika. They arrived at the top together, immediately dropping back a few steps as bullets whizzed past their ears and knocked dust and plaster off the walls behind them.

Mika eased up to the landing, her rifle in front of her, her finger on the trigger guard, ready to return fire.

Lance slipped up beside her. "Cover me." He flung himself out onto the second-floor landing, rolled onto his belly and kept his head low as one man fired at him while the other frantically attempted to fit a key into a door handle. Lance aimed his rifle at the man firing at him. Before he could pull the trigger, the man jerked backward and fell to the floor.

The one struggling with the door handle dropped

the key and swung around, raising a handgun toward them.

Lance fired, taking him down with his first shot.

Mika raced forward, snatched the key from the floor, shoved it into the lock, twisted and flung open the door.

A Hamas soldier, wearing a black hood that covered his head, face and neck, with only his eyes visible, held a handgun to an older man's temple and shouted in Arabic.

"He says he will kill Yaron if we get any closer," Mika said. She spoke in Arabic to the man, her tone demanding.

The man's eyes narrowed, and he said something that sounded like he was spitting the words at her, apparently angry that a woman dared to demand anything from him.

The captive diplomat's eyes widened, and his entire body trembled. A moment later, his knees buckled, and he fell toward the floor.

His captor struggled to hold the man's body up in front of him, failing miserably. The pistol he held at the man's temple shifted away from the Deputy Minister's face as he collapsed.

The Hamas soldier lost his grip. Letting go of his hostage, he raised his pistol toward Mika.

Lance fired, hitting the man in the chest.

The man's gun slipped from his fingers and clattered against the floor. He clutched his chest, his hand coming away covered in his own blood. The soldier stared across at Mika and choked out a gurgling, "Allahu Akbar." He fell forward like a cut tree, hitting the floor with a resounding thud and lying still.

Mika knelt beside Yaron, speaking urgently in Hebrew.

"We have Yaron," Lance reported.

"Get him the hell out of here. We have more company coming," Ketchum said into Lance's ear.

Lance bent down beside Mika, draped one of Yaron's arms over his shoulder and wrapped his arm around the man's waist.

Mika did the same on the other side.

"Ready…up." Lance straightened, taking most of the man's weight.

Yaron wasn't a huge man, but he also wasn't conscious.

"Can you steady him for just a moment," Lance asked.

Mika planted her feet apart and shifted Yaron's weight against her.

Lance released the man then slung him over his shoulder in a fireman's carry. "Let's go."

Mika assumed point, moving swiftly ahead of Lance, her weapon at the ready.

They descended the stairs slower than Lance would have liked due to the narrowness of the stairwell and the weight he carried.

Thankfully, the gunfire had ceased on the main floor.

Ketchum met them at the bottom of the stairs. "Alpha Team is taking fire. Once we get Yaron out of the village, they can fall back to the extraction point."

"The sooner we make that happen, the better," Lance said.

"Let me get on one side," Ketchum said.

Lance shook his head. "Just lead the way and get someone to cover my six. I'll get him to the extraction point."

Ketchum issued orders.

Mika led the way out the back door of the building and through a maze of streets between the damaged structures, finally emerging in an open area on the edge of the small, abandoned town.

The field was empty, but not for long. The thumping of rotor blades filled the air.

Lance's shoulders strained with the weight of his burden.

Yaron groaned and pushed his hands against Lance's back, muttering in Hebrew.

"He wants you to put him down," Mika said.

Lance wanted the same.

"Don't do it," Mika said. "The helicopter is almost here."

The muscles in his shoulders burning, Lance counted the seconds as the first helicopter touched down.

"Get Yaron on board and go," Ketchum said into Lance's headset.

Lance lurched forward, striding as fast as he could. When he reached the Black Hawk, he dumped the diplomat onto the floor of the chopper. He turned, grabbed Mika around the waist and swung her up into the aircraft. Her two male counterparts, who'd covered them as they'd run across the field, climbed aboard with her.

Lance waved to the door gunner. "Go, go, go, go!" he spoke into his headset to the pilot, and the helicopter rose into the air.

"Get in!" Mika leaned toward him and started to get out of the craft.

He shook his head. "You have to stay with him. Finish your mission." Lance turned away and ran back to help the others extricate themselves from Hamas.

Alpha Team had taken up positions to provide cover as Bravo Team fell back, each man making his way to the extraction point as quickly as possible.

"Got a man down," a voice said into the headset.

"How far away from the extraction point?" Ketchum asked.

"One block. I can see the clearing ahead, but we're taking fire."

"I'm going in." Lance jogged back into the village.

"I'm with you." Smoke fell in beside Lance.

"Not without me." Ice brought up the rear. "Got your back."

The three men ran toward the gunfire.

When they located the two men pinned in by enemy fire, they put their training to work.

"I have a clear shot of one of them," Gonzo said into Lance's headset. "Taking it."

A Hamas soldier fell from his concealed location atop a damaged building onto the street below.

Lance shifted his night-vision goggles into place and studied the streets and ruined buildings around him. A flash of green movement caught his attention. Another flash and he was certain.

A Hamas militant stood on the other side of a low, crumbling wall. Each time, he stood, fired and dropped back down behind what was left of a wall.

Lance waited for the man to pop up again. When he did, Lance nailed him. "Cover me while I get in to help."

"Smoke and Gonzo, it's on you two. Cover us," Ice said.

Lance left the corner of a destroyed building and raced toward the opposite side of the road to where the two Deltas were holed up behind a four-foot-high section of wall that remained from someone's home. Bullets flew around him. As soon as he passed the stone wall, he dropped behind it.

One of the Deltas was down, his leg almost as damaged as the wall they hid behind.

"Can you put any weight on that leg?"

The Delta winced. "If I could, I'd get myself out of here."

With his muscles still burning after carrying the diplomat, Lance bent to lift the man in a fireman's hold. However, Ice appeared beside him before he could.

"You get one side," Ice said. "I'll get the other." To the man on the ground, he said. "Buddy, hold on the best you can. We're going to move fast."

"Roger," the Delta gritted out.

Draping the man's arms over their shoulders, Ice and Lance lifted him and started running what felt like the longest yards toward the helicopter descending in the clearing.

With the first helicopter already gone with a light load, the second one would take the rest of Alpha and Bravo team out.

The teams loaded up.

Ketchum, Smoke and two IDF soldiers provided cover fire while the men leaped on board. When Ice and Lance arrived at the aircraft, hands reached out and dragged the injured man aboard.

The last four men backed toward the chopper, firing as they did.

"Get in!" the door gunner shouted. "I've got it from here." The men turned and scrambled aboard the crowded helicopter.

The gunner unleashed the fury of his machine

gun on the Hamas men firing at them as the chopper left the ground and rose over the top of the ridge and out of range of the enemy below.

Not until they were well away from the gunfire did Lance relax and remember to breathe. When he did, he thought about his brave Israeli partner and wondered if she and the Deputy Defense Minister had made it back to the base all right.

He hoped he'd see her when they landed. Something in her eyes and her demeanor had him wanting to know more about the woman who ran toward danger instead of away from it.

When they landed, he was disappointed to discover Mika and the minister had already gone.

Not only had he missed her, but he was also hustled to the hotel where the other Deltas were temporarily housed. He'd be on standby for the first available plane back to Texas. With no idea how long that would be, he doubted he'd have time to locate the woman whose courage and determination had captured his imagination. He was intrigued and wanted more time to get to know her.

Once he was back in Texas, there would be little chance of meeting her again. They lived on two different continents and were married to their services in their respective countries.

Still...he would have liked to get to know her better and discover if her lips were as soft as they'd appeared.

CHAPTER 3

MIKA BLUE TRAVELED with Efraim Yaron in the helicopter to a secure landing location near Jerusalem, where an ambulance waited to transport Yaron from the helicopter to one of the most advanced hospitals in the city. Mika had orders to accompany Yaron until she was relieved of her duties by her commanding officer.

Yaron received treatment for minor cuts and dehydration, was given a bag of IV fluids and kept overnight.

Mika stood guard outside his door throughout the night. By morning, she was exhausted and ready to shoot someone for a cup of coffee. No one had stopped her from carrying her rifle into the hospital. She grinned. Most hospital staff gave her a wide berth when they passed her in the hallway.

The doctors and nurses were going over his

discharge instructions when Mika's commander arrived.

"There's a transport vehicle outside waiting to return you to the base. Pack a bag and go home. You have the next two weeks off."

Mika frowned. "I don't need that much time to recuperate, sir," she said.

"You've done well. You deserve the time. Go home, visit your father. Go fishing. You did say you like to fish, didn't you?"

She nodded, her frown deepening.

Her commander's brow furrowed as he looked at her. "Do you even know how to relax?"

He had a point. She hadn't taken a vacation in years, preferring to train and conduct missions with her Sayeret Matkal unit. They were her family away from home. Besides, her father was busier in his retirement than he'd been on active duty. Still, she hadn't seen him in months, and it would be good to surprise him with a visit.

"Thank you, sir." With one last glance at the government official she'd help rescue, she studied Yaron. He had a reputation of being aggressive and volatile. He didn't appear at all aggressive now. Judging by the bruises on his face, Hamas had beaten the aggression out of him. Mika left the hospital, climbed into the waiting military vehicle and leaned back against the seat for the duration of the trip back to her quarters. Once there, she showered, dressed in civilian trousers and a pullover knit shirt in a soft light blue. Pulling her hair back in a ponytail at the base of her nape, she packed a bag, checked her watch and headed for her car.

The drive to her father's house usually took less than an hour. That bright, sunny day it took longer with heavy traffic on the roads. By the time she reached his place, she was so tired she could barely keep her eyes open. Her father wasn't home, and she hadn't expected him to be. She had a key to his house and was always welcome. She let herself in, dropped her suitcase in the spare bedroom, kicked off her shoes and collapsed on the bed.

In less than a minute, she was sound asleep.

WHAT FELT LIKE SECONDS LATER, a voice called out from the doorway, "Do you want to eat or sleep through dinner?"

Mika's eyes blinked open.

Daniel Blum leaned against the doorframe, his arms crossed over his chest. He might be in his fifties, but he was still a handsome man despite his graying temples. She could understand how her mother had fallen for him, given up her life in the States, and stayed in Israel to be his wife. His face and demeanor were very dear to Mika. She really needed to make more time to be with him.

"Hello, Aba," she said, using the English greeting

and the Hebrew word for father. Until she was six, she'd used a combination of English and Hebrew in her parent's home. Her father hadn't changed that habit after the death of her mother. He liked hearing her speak English. It reminded him of his beloved wife. The man had never remarried.

She sat up and swung her legs over the side of the bed.

"Difficult mission?" he asked, leading the way to the kitchen, where he poured a cup of coffee for his daughter.

She nodded.

He handed her the mug of steaming brew. "Will you be here long?"

She smiled. "Already trying to get rid of me?"

With a crooked grin, he shook his head. "Not at all. I enjoy your visits. They seem to be fewer and farther between."

A twinge of guilt tugged at her gut. "I've been busy."

"Same," he said. "But it's about time you came home."

She cocked an eyebrow. "You know the road goes both ways."

His lips twisted in a wry grin. "I know, but your apartment isn't nearly as comfortable as this house."

She set her cup on the counter and wrapped her arms around her father. "I missed you."

"I missed you too, daughter." He engulfed her in a tight hug.

When they broke apart, she grabbed her coffee, and he turned on the television to the news channel. As they worked together to prepare a meal, they commented on the happenings throughout the country.

When a reporter appeared in front of the hospital Mika had left hours before, she leaned forward. "Could you please turn up the volume?"

Her father adjusted the set.

The reporter approached the man Mika and the highly skilled team of special operations forces had extracted from Palestinian-held territory less than twenty-four hours earlier. "Breaking news," he said. "Deputy Defense Minister Efraim Yaron was rescued last night in a daring raid into Palestinian territory. After a brief stay in the hospital, he's being released to return to his duties." The man turned toward the hospital entrance. "And here he comes now. Minister Yaron," the reporter called out, "how was it to be captured by Hamas and held captive for so many days?"

Seated in a wheelchair, the Deputy Defense Minister allowed the orderly to push him past the door and bring him to a halt at the curb. Bracing his hands on the arms of the wheelchair, Yaron pushed to his feet and lifted his chin. "Unacceptable," he responded, his lips curled into a snarl. "I will not be abused in such a way and stand by and do nothing."

The reporter shoved the microphone into Yaron's face. "Sir, will Hamas suffer any repercussions for detaining you?"

Yaron's eyebrows dipped low on his forehead, and his mouth and jaw tightened into grim lines. "We cannot afford to let terrorists rob our citizens of their freedom with their sole reason being they do not believe in the same religion or political ideology."

"Deputy Minister, will there be repercussions?" the reporter persisted.

Yaron's eyes narrowed. "Mark my words—there will be repercussions." He pushed through the crowd of reporters and people surrounding him and climbed into a waiting limousine.

Mika crossed to the television and turned down the volume. "What do you think Yaron will do?"

Her father's brow dipped into deep frown lines. "With Yaron, you can count on fireworks. He loves drone bombings and isn't afraid to deploy them. He was the official who ordered the bombing of a Palestinian village near the West Bank. Twenty men, women and children died in that bombing. I've never met someone with so little regard for human life."

"And we helped to save his sorry ass." Mika snorted softly. "Let's hope he learned some lessons about kindness during captivity."

Her father shook his head. "Some men don't change, even after suffering in adverse conditions."

"You think Yaron is one of those men?"

He shrugged as he opened the refrigerator door and stared inside. "We shall see."

A shiver snaked down Mika's spine. With Yaron promising retribution, it was only a matter of time.

"We have two choices for dinner..." her father said, changing the subject.

Mika grinned. "And they are...?"

The retired soldier returned her smile. "Pizza delivery and pizza delivery."

"Tough decision," Mika said, tapping her chin. "Pizza it is."

"I would've thought you'd prefer something lighter, like a salad."

Mika snorted. "Since when have you known me to settle for just a salad for dinner?" She worked hard and ate the calories she needed to meet the physical demands of her job.

"How long are you off work?" her father asked as he entered the phone number to order pizza.

"Two weeks. I could take more if I like. I haven't taken leave in over two years." She stared out the window at the small back patio, not seeing the sunshine or furniture. Instead, she saw the face of the Delta Force operator who'd been her partner the night before. She found herself thinking about Texas.

Mika turned to her father. "Did you ever visit mama's hometown?"

His eyebrows met in a V. "Once," he said. "Why?"

"I've been thinking about Texas. Would it be crazy if I scheduled a trip back to the states during my time off?"

Her father looked around the kitchen. "And leave all this excitement?" He smiled. "Other than for missions, you've never left Israel, except when you attended the university in Austin. You should consider it."

Her lips twisted. "Or I could stay and visit with my favorite man."

Her father's brow dipped lower. "You can't count on me being here forever. You need to find a man with whom you can share your life."

"Ha," she said. "What man would love a woman who can outrun, outshoot and probably outfight him in hand-to-hand combat?"

"Lots of men," her father answered and winced.

She tilted her head and raised an eyebrow. "Really?"

"I love you," he said.

"You have to." She crossed the kitchen and hugged him tightly. "You're my father. Most men are intimidated by a woman who can clearly kick their asses."

He held her at arm's length for a moment and then dropped his hold on her to retrieve his coffee mug. "Maybe you shouldn't advertise that you can kick a man's ass."

"See? You admit it. Men are easily intimidated. I don't have a chance of getting to know one because my manly body and attitude would turn him off."

Her father had been in the middle of sipping his coffee when she'd spoken. Her words made him spew the hot fluid. "Manly body?" He laughed out loud. When he realized she was not laughing with him, he set his cup on the counter and rested his palm against her cheek. "*Yekirati*," he spoke the term of endearment softly, "you look nothing like a man. You are as beautiful as your mother."

Her heart swelled. She covered her father's hand with her own. "Thank you. Working with men, I have to pretend I'm one of them."

"You may be as strong, brave and skilled as your counterparts, but you are not a man, by any means." He kissed her forehead. "There is someone special out there who will see you for the person you are inside."

An image of the Delta Force soldier flashed through her mind. She shook her head.

"You should go to America," her father said. "Take a real vacation. You've earned it."

She turned and paced across the kitchen. "That kind of trip takes a lot of planning. It's not something one does on impulse."

"It's not something *you* would do on impulse." Her father chuckled. "So, be impulsive. Go somewhere. You're young, healthy and, most importantly, not tied down by a husband and children. Now is the time to be impulsive."

She sighed. "I'll think about it."

"Don't use up all of your leave thinking about it," he warned.

She turned to him, her mouth twisting. "I would've thought you'd want me to stay here with you."

"There is nothing I'd like better. But you need to live your life, have adventures…fall in love."

She laughed. "You make it sound easy. I'm in the Sayeret Matkal. The military *is* our life. We're married to it."

Her father shook his head. "I want you to have what I had with your mother." He held his arms open.

"She died and broke your heart." Mika stepped into her father's embrace. "Why would you want me to suffer a broken heart?"

"Knowing now that we would only have a few short years together, I would do it all over again," he whispered.

"But you were heartbroken, and, as far as I can tell, you still are." She leaned her cheek against his chest, her own heart hurting for her father.

"I loved your mother so much. Yes, it hurt when

she left us, but I cherish her memory every day and thank the Lord that I had what time I did with her." He leaned back and stared down into her eyes. "And she gave me a gift that would remind me of her for the rest of my life." He touched the tip of her nose. "You."

Here in the home where she'd grown up, with her father holding her close, was the only place she felt she could let down her guard and be something other than a highly trained fighting machine. With her father, she was a child, a girl, a young woman but not a soldier.

"You've spent the past eight years dedicating your life to your country. Take some time to do something for yourself." He stroked her hair once more then set her away. "If I don't get that pizza ordered, we'll starve."

If she wasn't mistaken, his eyes were glassy, full of moisture. The man who had hidden emotions from his subordinates for the twenty-eight years he'd served in the IDF would not let his daughter see him cry.

"I'll order pizza," he said, "if you'll go online and see what flights are available to the States."

The more she thought about it, the more she leaned toward the idea of making a trip to America. She hadn't been back since she'd graduated. She had leave to burn. Why not?

She met her father's gaze. "Why don't you come with me?"

He shook his head. "I have meetings scheduled through this week and next, or I would."

"Cancel them," she urged.

His lips pressed together. "I can't. I committed to them weeks ago. Don't you have a friend who can go with you?"

Her only friends were her teammates in the special forces. All male, many of them married or in relationships. "No."

"Don't you have some old college friends you can visit stateside?"

"It's been a long time, and I haven't kept in touch."

Most of her friends from college had gone on to marry and have children. They were busy in a stage of life Mika couldn't relate with. Somewhere in the back of her mind, she hoped one day she might.

There was someone she wouldn't mind seeing again…

The idea slipped into her thoughts as it had done many times since the night before.

She thought of Lance Rankin, the Delta Force operative who lived close to where her mother grew up. If she chose to spend her vacation in Texas, what were the chances she'd run into the man?

It would never happen. She didn't know where he lived, didn't have his phone number or even the name of his unit at Fort Hood. It wasn't like she'd run into him. If she wanted to see him, she'd have to do some digging to find him. He'd mentioned renting a cabin on a lake. He'd also mentioned a bar his team used as a hangout.

Her eyes narrowed. What had he called it? Something Dog…Salty Dog!

A flash of excitement surged through her at the thought of finding Lance.

If she did, would he *want* to see her? What would she say?

Hi. Remember me? We met in a helicopter just a few days ago. Want to get a beer and hang out?

Like one of the guys. To him, that's what she was. One of the members of a temporary military team organized for a one-time joint mission.

The few minutes she'd had to talk with him hadn't given him a clue as to who she was beneath the uniform and had only given her a glimpse of the man she'd been partnered with because he'd been in battle with females before.

Still…a trip to Texas would be something completely different from Israel. For old times' sake, she could visit the university campus and drive by her mother's old house in Salado. As well, a trip down to San Antonio to hang out on the River Walk would be fun. She'd always wanted to visit the wineries near Fredericksburg or hike up to the top of Enchanted Rock north of there. She wouldn't be bored.

Lonely, maybe…but not bored.

"I'll look at flights," she said softly.

Her father grinned. "Great! I'll order pizza."

While her father called for pizza delivery, Mika went to her room, dug her tablet out of her suitcase and carried it back to the kitchen.

Her father ended his call. "Pizza will be here in thirty minutes. That should give you time to book a seat on an airline." He pulled out a chair at the table. "Sit. Let's see what flights are available."

She chuckled and dropped into the chair he proffered. "Are you sure you don't want to cancel some meetings and go with me?"

"I'd love to go, but I can't. This will be your grand adventure." He pulled up a chair beside her. "You might meet someone special. In that event, you won't want your father tagging along."

"I'll always want you around," she said, leaning against his shoulder.

"I won't always be around, Mika." He stared into her eyes. "You need to have a life of your own."

Her chest tightened at the thought of losing him. He was her only family. "I thought that's what I was doing in the Army."

"You need a family of your own."

"My team is my family."

He nodded. "Brothers. You need a husband and children."

"What if I don't want either?"

Her father drew in a slow, deep breath and let it out. "That is your choice. I would hope that you don't deprive yourself of love. It is the most fulfilling aspect of life." For a long time, he held her gaze. "Is that it? You don't want a husband and children?"

She wanted to tell him no, but it would be a lie. "Yes. Someday."

Her father's lips curved at the corners before he glanced toward her tablet. "Where do you want to go?"

"Texas."

He cocked an eyebrow. "Not California, Florida or New York? You don't have to go to America. You could go to Canada, Europe or South Africa."

"I'm looking at this as a spontaneous with little planning or preparation trip," she reasoned. "I'm familiar with Texas. I'll go there."

While they waited for the pizza to be delivered, Mika and her father found a flight leaving at midnight the next day and arriving midday in Dallas the following day.

Mika's finger hovered over the button to book the flight.

"What else would you do if you stayed here?" her father asked, arching an eyebrow.

"Visit with the only man I ever loved," she murmured, still holding her finger over the button.

"And be bored in less than a day," he said. "As much as I like having you here, I'd be happier knowing you were having an adventure, meeting new people, and maybe, finding someone with whom you'd consider spending the rest of your life."

Mika laughed out loud. "People don't fall in love in two weeks." Though the thought made her pulse quicken. Ever since she'd turned twenty-nine, she'd felt restless, as if she needed something else in her life she didn't already have, and that time was running out, which was ridiculous. She had a lot more life left to live in her young body. But her child-bearing years were more limited. If she wanted to have children, she needed to get started within the next few years.

"I met your mother when I went to Texas for a two-week training exercise with the US. I had dinner at one restaurant every evening after training. By the time I left for home, I knew I'd marry your mother. It took two months of exchanging letters and phone calls before I was able to get back to Texas to ask her to marry me."

"Mother told me about that." Mika touched her father's hand. "She said it was love at first sight for her but that it took two and a half months for you to come to your senses."

His smile was sweet and sad. "I knew I would marry her the night we met. It took me two and a half months to arrange a ring and a proper proposal. I also had to research the legal implications of marrying a foreigner and bringing her back with me to Israel. Thankfully, she got her passport before I got back. We were married within the week and flew back to Israel as husband and wife."

Her father's gaze looked past her to somewhere on the wall. He wasn't seeing her or the wall. By the slight smile on his lips, he was somewhere else. Perhaps, a different time.

"Let me be clear," Mika said. "I'm not going to America to find a husband."

"Of course not," her father said. "But if you do meet someone, be open to the possibilities."

She rolled her eyes. "Fine."

"Then you're going?" he asked.

"Still thinking," she stalled.

He reached across the table and laid his hand over hers, pressing it, and the finger hovering over the enter key, down.

A combination of fear and excitement rippled throughout her body as the booking formation screen appeared. She was booked on a flight leaving the next night for Texas.

Her father leaned back, a smug smile on his face. "Now, that wasn't so hard, was it?"

It was positively terrifying.

She was going to Texas.

Hell…she had to pack!

With a little more than twenty-four hours to pack and make the hour-long drive to the Tel Aviv airport, she had plenty of time to prepare.

Then why was she so damn nervous?

She wasn't afraid of flying on airplanes. Even those crossing oceans. Nor was she afraid of traveling alone.

No. It wasn't the trip making her shake all over. It was the fact that she'd already made up her mind to look up Lance Rankin.

CHAPTER 4

Mika barely slept that night. After receiving clearance from her commanding officer to leave the country, she'd dug out her passport and made reservations for a rental car for when she arrived in Dallas. She hadn't made hotel reservations, preferring to make that decision when she got to the area around Fort Hood. She might lose her nerve and spend the night in Waco. Fearless in battle, she was frightfully inept at social situations.

She was up before her father, had the coffee made and breakfast cooking when he entered the kitchen in a hurry.

"I have an early-morning meeting I can't be late for." He kissed her forehead, took the mug of coffee she handed to him and headed for the door.

"Will I see you before I leave for the airport?" she asked.

"Yes, of course. I wouldn't miss your send-off." He stopped, turned around and went back to where she was standing. "Just in case, give your old father a hug." He set the coffee mug on the counter and folded her into his arms.

She wrapped her own arms around his waist and squeezed tight. "I love you, Aba," she whispered.

"I love you, too," he said. "Always remember that. No matter what happens, who you meet or where you end up living."

She laughed and looked up into his eyes. "You act as if I plan on staying in the States."

"If you meet the right person, it could happen."

"I couldn't live there. Not if you're still here."

"I won't always be here, *Yekirati*. You have to follow your heart."

"My heart is here with you," she insisted. "You are my family."

"For now." He stepped back, cupped her cheeks in his palms and pressed a kiss to her forehead. "I love you and want the best for my only child."

"How can any man live up to your example?" she asked. "I wouldn't be the person I am if not for you. No one will ever love me as you do."

"Someone will love you for the strong, brave woman you are." He smiled down at her. "No matter where you are, remember I will always love you."

"And I will always love you." She gave him a quick hug, her eyes filling with tears she didn't want him to see. "Go before you're late for your meeting."

After her father left for work, Mika switched on the television only to find a news reporter standing in front of the rubble of a building. The caption below the image indicated the building was in the West Bank area of Palestinian territory.

The reporter spoke in Arabic. "The death toll is up to fifty, with more missing and injured. Killed in this senseless attack by the Israeli government were the wife and children of Khaled Aziz, the leader of the Hamas militant group that captured Deputy Defense Minister Yaron." The reporter's eyes narrowed, and he touched a hand to the radio in his ear. He looked up, his eyes widening. "We have a video prepared by Khaled Aziz himself."

A few seconds later, a man with dark eyes, thick eyebrows and silvery-white hair and beard appeared on the television.

"Efraim Yaron is responsible for the deaths of women and children. For my family." He raised his finger, pointing it at the camera, his face tense, his gaze piercing, looking straight into Mika's soul. "I will take from him what he took from me. I will take the same from each member of the team who crossed into Palestine to free him so that he could perform such atrocities. Their families will suffer, and they will die as they have murdered our women and children."

A shiver slithered across Mika's skin. The Hamas leader could have been standing there in front of her, his message clear and threatening. He would go after everyone responsible for freeing Yaron, allowing him to kill Palestinians. What worried her more was that he'd vowed to kill the families as well.

Mika picked up her cellphone and called her father.

He didn't answer, probably due to the heavy traffic on his way to the government building where he worked.

She texted him a message, telling him to watch Aziz's video and be careful.

For the rest of the day, she alternated between pacing the floor of her father's home, packing for a trip she wasn't sure she should take and watching the news for updates on the bombing in the West Bank.

Near the end of the day, about the time her father would be on his way home, a news flash interrupted the regular programming. A home in a Jerusalem suburb had exploded with a family inside. A woman and her three children were killed. They were identified as the family of a member of the Israeli Defense Force. While the reporter stood in front of the burned-out home, a man burst through the barricades keeping the public away from the scene. He wore a military uniform and ran toward the home. When firefighters stepped into his path, he fought his way through, only stopping when he reached the smoldering remains of what had once been a house. The cameraman followed his movements, the reporter commenting as the man shoved his hands through his hair, anguish making his face haggard and drawn.

A loud crack sounded in the background.

Firefighters and the reporter dropped to the ground. The camera jerked and tilted as the cameraman got down. When he righted the camera, the reporter continued to describe the scene.

"That was the sound of gunfire," the report said, his voice shaking. He lifted his head and looked around. "I can't tell if anyone was hit…"

The camera panned the area, coming to rest on the front of the destroyed home. The man who'd been standing there lay on the ground, unmoving.

When no other shots rang out, people began to move. A firefighter, hunkering low, ran toward the man on the ground in front of the house and knelt beside him, touching his fingers to the base of the man's throat. He turned him over onto his back and shook his head.

The cameraman zoomed in on the man in the military uniform. What had once been his chest was now a gaping, bloody hole.

Mika gasped, recognizing the man's face. He'd been a member of her team. A highly trained Sayeret Matkal operative who'd been an integral part of the team who'd freed Deputy Defense Minister Yaron.

The cameraman swung back to the reporter.

"We just received word a similar explosion occurred in another area of the city. The first responders have confirmed three deaths in that incident…a woman and two small children." The reporter frowned, touching a hand to his headset. "I understand there is a video from Hamas leader Khaled Aziz referencing the bombings."

The image on the television screen switched to the silver-haired militant leader.

He stared straight at the camera and spoke. "You reap what you sow."

Mika's blood ran cold. A moment later, her cellphone rang.

She grabbed it and stared down at the caller ID.

It was her commander.

"Yes, sir," she answered.

"The homes of two members of our team have been targeted. Leave your place now and warn your family they could be next."

Her heart racing, she ran through the house and slung her bag onto the bed. "Thank you for the warning," she said as she gathered her things. "What about the Americans? Should they be worried?"

"Anyone who was involved in freeing Yaron should be concerned."

Mika ran into the bathroom and grabbed her toothbrush. "Have they been warned?"

"Not yet."

Her heart skipped several beats. The Americans could be targeted as well as the Israelis. "Where are they quartered?"

He gave her the name of the hotel. "I'll notify Ketchum. He can pass on the word to the other members of his team."

"I'll pray for the team," she said. "Khaled means to fulfill his promise."

"Pack a bag and get moving, but keep your cellphone charged," her commander said. "We're organizing a team to locate Khaled."

"Yes, sir," she said. "Stay safe in the meantime."

"You, too."

As soon as the call ended, Mika tried contacting her father again.

He answered on the first ring. "Mika, get out of the house."

"I'm packing now."

"You might not have time to pack. Just get out," he insisted. "I'm on my way now. You need to get to Tel Aviv and on that plane to America."

"Aba," she said, coming to a stop in front of her bag, her pulse slowing the thoughts that were becoming clearer. "I can't go to America."

"Yes. You can." He paused. When she didn't say anything, he went on. "Khaled will kill you and everyone involved in that raid to free Yaron."

"Then we have to take out Khaled," she said, her voice low and firm. "Cut off the head of the snake, and the rest will die. Until he's dead, none of us will be safe."

"I'm sure there's nothing I can do to talk you out of this," her father said.

"No, sir," she said, her heart beating steadily, her decision made. "I have a job to do. I'd feel better if you drove to Tel Aviv and took my seat on the plane to America. With you safely out of the country, I can focus on what needs to be done."

"I'm not going," her father said.

"If you don't go, Khaled will find and kill you."

"I was a member of the IDF. I know how to be careful," her father insisted.

"And Khaled will make certain I suffer by forcing me to watch you die at his hand." Her heart would break into a million pieces if her father died, especially if he died because of his daughter's role in an extraction. "Please, Aba, go to America. I need to devote my attention to taking Khaled out of action. The sooner, the better, before he targets more women and children."

"I'm on my way home now. I'll be there in a few minutes."

"No, Aba, don't come here. Khaled is bombing the homes of my teammates. He will not hesitate to target this address. His people could be outside right now."

"Then get out," her father said, his tone insistent.

"I am." She put the phone on speaker, dropped it

on the bed and zipped her bag. "I'm on my way out the door now. Is there anything you want me to take out of here?"

"You. Just get yourself out," he said. "Mika, go."

She slung her bag over her shoulder, grabbed her phone and ran through the house. She'd almost made it to the door when she spotted the photograph of her family on a table beside the living room sofa. Making a quick detour, she snatched the picture frame, dug the family photo album out from the bottom shelf of the end table, and turned back to the door. As she neared it, she saw a dark vehicle slow to a halt in front of the house.

Mika's heart turned a somersault in her chest. She spun on her heels and sprinted for the back door.

She twisted the handle, flung open the door and ran out, slamming into the solid wall of a man's chest.

Arms came up around her.

She started to fight, but a familiar voice sounded in her ear.

"Mika, it's me, Lance. We need to get you out of here."

She looked up into the man's face. For a split second, a rush of relief washed over her.

The sound of glass shattering behind her pushed relief out and filled her with urgency. "Get down!" she yelled and pushed him away from the door, pulling it shut behind her.

Lance grabbed her and shoved her to the ground, throwing his body over hers. The house exploded behind them, sending glass, plaster and splintered wood shooting like missiles through the air.

The concussion made Mika's ears ring, and she could barely breathe.

As soon as the explosion was over, Lance rolled over and knelt beside her. "Are you all right?" he asked.

With his heavy weight off her body, she could drag air into her lungs. "Yes." His voice and her own sounded as if they were coming from a long way down a dark tunnel, warring with a piercing ringing sound.

Leaping to his feet, Lance reached down to take her hand. "We need to get out of here before they realize no one was inside." He pulled her to her feet, wrapping one arm around her waist to steady her. Then he took her hand and started to run.

She dug in her heels. "Wait." With the bag still slung over her shoulder, she scooped up the photo frame and album.

The dust was just beginning to settle when they ducked between houses behind her father's destroyed home.

Mika glanced back once at the house she'd grown up in, her heart squeezing hard in her chest. There would be no more visits home. The house she and her father had shared with her mother was gone.

Mika's eyes filled with tears. She turned away from her past and stumbled.

Lance's arm came up around her, strong and firm, giving her the support she needed until she regained her balance.

His hand dropped from the small of her back to clasp hers inside his. "Got this?"

She nodded.

They took off running away from the wreckage of what once had been her home.

Her heart hurt for the loss. It had been her last connection with the mother she'd lost so long ago, and it was the one place she'd always known she could come home to. She was thankful her father had not been home at the time of the explosion. Had he not had a meeting that day, he would have been there, and so would she. Khaled would have killed two birds with one mortar round.

A block away from the destruction, Lance came to a stop beside an SUV, pulled open the passenger door and tilted his head. "Get in."

She frowned as she hesitated. "Shouldn't I drive? I know these streets better than you do."

He shrugged. "Good point, as long as we move out quickly." He tossed her the key fob and got into the passenger seat.

Mika rounded to the driver's side, climbed in and started the engine.

Lance sat sideways in his seat, glancing back over

his shoulder. "You might want to step on it. There's a vehicle turning onto this street.

She glanced in the rearview mirror, her heart skipping several beats as she recognized the dark sedan that had slowed outside her house seconds before the explosion. Mika slammed her foot down on the accelerator. The SUV leaped forward, burning a layer of rubber off the tires as she spun out and away from the curb.

The dark sedan behind them sped up, closing the distance between them.

Mika had been right about taking the driver's seat. She knew the roads in her family home's neighborhood. At the next corner, she made a sharp left, and then raced to the end of that street and turned right.

"Still back there," Lance said.

Her eyes narrowed and her foot pushed hard on the accelerator. She barely slowed at the next corner, making a swift left. Before she'd gone half a block, she pulled into an alley, zigzagged past trash bins and eased out onto another street.

"I don't think they saw you duck into the alley. I didn't see the black car at all."

Could they have ditched their tail so soon?

As she pulled out of the alley, she glanced right in time to see a dark car round the corner at the end of the street and charge toward them.

Mika spun the steering wheel left and gave the

SUV all the gas it would take, once again burning rubber in her effort to lose the vehicle following them.

She raced away from the subdivision and out onto a major thoroughfare, passing vehicles on the right and then on the left. At one point, she drove up onto a sidewalk to get around stalled traffic.

No matter how fast and furiously she drove, she couldn't seem to shake the car behind her.

As the light in front of her turned red, Mika knew she had to do something drastic to lose the sedan.

"There," Lance pointed down a street to their right. A large cargo truck was backing out of a tight space, moving slowly.

Mika ran the red light, whipped around two cars slowing to let the truck back out into the street.

Mika didn't hesitate. She raced around the stopped cars and blew through the narrow gap between the rear end of the backing truck and the wall of a building. She clipped a trash bin, sending it spinning.

The truck continued backing up, completely blocking the street long enough for Mika to get to the end and turn.

"The truck's still blocking them." Lance spun in his seat and alternated between looking ahead and staring down at the map on his cellphone. "Turn right at the next corner. That should lead you onto the expressway."

Taking the corner fast, the SUV's rear tires skidded sideways. The tires engaged, and they pushed forward, finding the way to the expressway, heavy with traffic, but moving.

Picking up speed, Mika wove through the cars.

"I don't see our tail," Lance said. "But keep going."

"I will, but I want to get off this road and into someplace we can hide."

"Agreed."

Without slowing, Mika looked for her opportunity to exit the expressway and drove into an industrial area. When she was certain they weren't followed, she pulled up behind an abandoned warehouse and stopped the SUV.

She pulled out her cellphone and dialed her father.

He answered on the first ring. "Thank the Lord," he said. "Tell me you're okay."

"I am," Mika said. "Tell me you aren't at the house."

"I was…at least what was left of it. I had to believe you made it out." His voice faltered.

"I drove past as the firefighters and police were arriving. I've been driving ever since, praying you would call."

"I'm okay," she said quietly. "We need to get you somewhere safe. As long as Khaled has his men targeting the team, our families are at risk."

"I won't hide," her father said. "I want to go after

Khaled and stop him before he hurts any more innocent women and children."

"Me too, Aba," she said. "But we have to gather our forces, protect our families and come up with a plan."

"Where are you?" her father asked.

"Safe for now. Meet me at the church where you and mother were married in twenty minutes," she said. "Disguise yourself and trust no one."

"What about you?" her father asked.

"I'll be there," she promised, her jaw hardening. "Please, Aba, be safe. You're all the family I have."

"And you are all I have," he replied.

Mika ended the call, wishing she didn't have to and afraid that it might be the last time she ever talked to her father.

She squared her shoulders and glanced across the console at Lance. "You realize you're in just as much danger as any of the Sayeret Matkal because of your role in freeing Yaron." She frowned. "Which reminds me. How did you find me?"

His lips quirked upward on the edges. "I asked around until I found out that you had gone to your father's. I kept asking until someone gave me an address. No one offered a phone number, or I would've called ahead. After the bombing yesterday and the Hamas leader claiming responsibility for it and threatening to kill all those involved, I figured I'd better look for you and make sure you were aware of what was going on."

Mika drew in what felt like the first deep breath she'd inhaled since seeing the dark sedan in front of her house. "Now would be a good time for you to fly home to the States," she said.

Lance shook his head. "That plane left this morning without me. I couldn't leave you and your team to defend yourselves and your families without helping. I was one of the people responsible for freeing Yaron. I couldn't bail and let you all bear the brunt of Khaled's revenge."

He clapped his hands together. "I'm hoping to get in on the mission to bring that asshat down. He's targeting women and children. I can't stand by and do nothing. In fact, I called in my team from back at Fort Hood. If we can get the Israeli government to ask for help, my team will be here as soon as they get the word."

Mika nodded. "We might need all the help we can get to find Khaled and bring him down."

CHAPTER 5

"We'll need to switch vehicles soon." Lance craned his neck, scanning all directions for potential threats. "The guys who were following us will have warned their buddies to be on the lookout for the make, model and license plate."

"We will. First, I want to get to my father and make sure he's safe." Her gaze remained on the road in front of her. She'd chosen to stay off the main highway running through Jerusalem and weave through the city streets to get to the church her mother had taken her to when she was little.

Lance's cellphone rang. The caller ID indicated Master Sergeant Ketchum. He answered immediately.

"Hack, you still with us?" Ketchum asked.

"Roger."

"You must have disappeared about the time all hell broke loose at the hotel."

Lance leaned forward. "What happened at the hotel?"

Mika shot a glance at him before returning her attention to the road.

"Most of us had gone out to breakfast. We were on our way back, and only a block away, when the front of the building exploded. From what we discovered, a suicide bomber showed up in the lobby. We accounted for all our guys and came up short when we looked for you. What happened?"

Lance stared across the console at Mika. "I put the two bombings together with Khaled's claim for revenge and figured Mika Blue would be one of the next targets."

"And?" Ketchum waited for his response.

"I'm with her now. Close call. Her home was destroyed."

"Damn. Sorry to hear that. Glad you got there before that happened."

"Not before...*as*."

"Fuck. You two okay? Do we need to send a security team to the hospital to provide protection?"

"No. We're okay, just residual ear ringing. We're on our way to connect with her family."

"They're not safe," Ketchum said.

"We know. She only has her father. He's prior military and knows the score."

"Like you, we saw what Khaled had to say and left the hotel before they saw that we weren't inside when their bomber cut loose. Basically, we're driving around town until we figure out what's next. We thought about catching a plane back to the states, but it didn't seem right to duck out when the going was getting tough for the Israelis we worked with on the mission to free Yaron."

"Exactly." Lance had gone with his gut, spoken with his Israeli contact, the man in charge of Mika, and got her family's home address. The man had been hesitant until the second bomb had gone off while Lance had been on the phone with him.

"There was another attack in the market square a few minutes ago," Ketchum said. "They followed the family of one of the Israeli special forces guys, his mother and his young, pregnant wife were killed by a suicide bomber, along with several other innocents. Dozens were injured. The shit's getting real. I have a call out to our Israeli contact, offering our support. I should hear back from him soon... Oh, wait. Got a call coming in now. Let me know when you have Mika's father."

"Roger." Lance ended the call.

Mika's mouth was set in a grim line.

"Did you hear any of that?" Lance asked.

She nodded. "Khaled has to be stopped."

"Along with all of the suicide bombers he's set loose in the city."

She shook her head. "We can't find all of them. We have to get to Khaled and make an example of him."

"Where is he?"

"We need our intelligence contacts to find him." She turned another corner and eased up to an intersection. "That's the church where my father will be waiting for us."

"Inside or in his car?" Lance asked.

"I'm not sure." A frown creased her brow as she turned away from the church and drove around the block. As they came around from the other side, she slowed and tipped her head toward a sleek, charcoal gray four-door sedan, pulled into a parking space beside the church. "That's his car."

They were still over fifty yards from the church and her father's vehicle.

"I can't tell if there's anyone in it." Mika eased forward.

Lance's gut tightened. "Stop."

Mika jammed on the brakes. "Why?"

"It doesn't feel right."

Before the last word left Lance's mouth, the sleek gray car exploded.

The blast shook their vehicle. Metal shrapnel pelted the hood and cracked the windshield.

"No!" Mika cried. She shoved open the driver's door, jumped out and ran toward the vehicle.

"Wait, Mika!" Lance called out. He reached into

the back seat, grabbed his handgun out of his go bag, slung the bag over his shoulder and raced after Mika. As he ran, he looked in all directions, high and low, for anyone who might be waiting for his opportunity to pick off the female soldier or himself.

Mika arrived at what was left of the vehicle—a mangled chassis, and not much else.

"Aba?" she said, her voice wobbling.

"Mika!" a shout rang out from around the side of the church. A tall man with olive skin and salt-and-pepper hair hurried toward her.

Lance raised his weapon, pointing it at the man.

"Aba!" Mika ran to the man and flung her arms around him. "I thought you were in the car."

He said something in Hebrew, smoothing a hand over her hair. He looked up at Lance, saw the gun in his hand and quickly pushed Mika behind him.

"It's okay, Aba," Mika said. "He's with me. This is Lance Rankin. He's an American. Lance, this is my father, Daniel Blum."

"Nice to meet you, and I don't mean to be rude, but we all need to get out of the open before someone takes a shot at us," Lance said. "Now."

He grabbed Mika's hand and ran into the church with her and her father.

Once inside, he called Ketchum. "Mika's father was just attacked. We're at a church about to leave. I'll drop a pin for our location when we get to a safe distance from here."

"We'll come get you as soon as you do. The Israelis are offering us a safe haven on the Israeli airbase for the time being. They're collecting the family members and bringing them in to protect them."

"Are they planning anything to stop this madness?" Lance asked.

"If not, we'll put our heads together," Ketchum said. "This can't continue."

"No shit," Lance glanced across the church at Mika talking softly with her father. "Get us to the base, and we'll come up with a plan."

"Good," Ketchum said. "The Israelis want our help. I just hope our government doesn't pull us back."

Lance frowned. "What are you hearing?"

"The guys who pull the strings aren't happy with what Yaron did, taking out that building with mortar fire. What Khaled is doing is equally wrong."

"Two wrongs don't make a right," Lance said.

"True. But they can't agree on a course of action. And we can't go rogue."

Couldn't they? After witnessing two explosions that had nearly taken his life and Mika's, he wasn't going to let the politicians pull him back. He'd go rogue, if he had to. He knew there might be consequences to his career in Delta Force and the Army.

Still, if that's what he had to do, he'd do it. He wouldn't leave Mika, her father, and the families of the Israeli special forces, high and dry without support and protection from terrorists. Khaled had started this whole thing by capturing and torturing Yaron.

Lance hoped his country would allow the Deltas already in Israel to help. Hell, they were in as much danger as any of Sayeret Matkal forces and their families. Until they left the country, they would be in danger. And leaving the country anytime soon was out of the question.

As soon as he ended the call with Ketchum, Lance met Mika's gaze. "We need to move before Khaled's men figure out they missed and come looking for us."

"Yes," she said. "We do." She nodded toward her father. "Ready?"

"Yes."

An old priest emerged from a door near the rear of the chapel and called out in Hebrew.

Mika's father answered in the same language. "He wants us to follow him. He says there is a secret passage that will get us out of here safely."

"You trust him?" Lance asked.

"Yes. He was the same priest who performed my marriage to Mika's mother thirty years ago."

Daniel Blum fell in step with the priest. Lance reached for Mika's hand.

She placed her palm in his and hurried after her father.

Lance couldn't help but notice how soft her hands

were. Soft but strong. She was decidedly feminine and totally capable of taking care of herself. Yet, she let him hold her hand and walk out of the church with her. He could get used to holding this woman's hand. He hoped he'd get the chance to do more of it. Lance couldn't regret missing that plane earlier that morning. If he had gone home to Texas, Mika and her father might not be alive at that moment.

If the Hamas terrorist, Khaled, had his way, none of the Israeli and American Special Forces personnel who'd been responsible for freeing Yaron would see the light of the next sunrise. He had to do something to keep that from happening.

MIKA HAD NEVER BEEN a female who liked to hold hands or have any kind of public displays of affection. She figured, as a woman, it only made her look weak in the eyes of her comrades and enemies. Frankly, she thought it was stupid to leave well-trained women on the sidelines when the men could do very little to make the situations any better. Women tended to think through multiple scenarios and to move quickly and decisively to achieve their goals. At least, she did.

The priest led them to the back of the church, through a door and down a set of stone stairs into a basement filled with old pews, boxes, crates and stacks of books. On the far side of the basement stood a bookshelf nestled against the wall. The old priest led them to the shelf and leaned his body against the side of it. The shelf shifted.

Lance dropped Mika's hand. "Let me," he said and took the priest's place. He pushed the shelf to the side, revealing an ancient passageway lined in stone.

Fishing his hand into the pocket of his black robe, the priest brought out a flashlight and handed it to Mika's father. "Safe passage to you."

"Thank you," Daniel Blum touched the priest's arm, turned and clicked the flashlight on. He led the way into the passage.

Mika and Lance followed.

Behind them, the priest pushed the bookshelf back in place, extinguishing the light behind them.

With only the flashlight beam guiding them, they followed the tunnel for several hundred feet before they came to a set of stairs leading upward. At the top, they encountered an old wooden door.

Daniel turned the knob and pushed it open a crack.

Daylight streamed through the opening through overhanging vines and brush.

"Let me go first," Mika said.

Her father shook his head. "I'm here. I'll go." He handed the flashlight back to her, shoved aside a layer of vines and stepped out of the tunnel into the open.

All Mika could see was the silhouette of her

father's legs as he stood above them. Then he turned and leaned into the opening. "It's safe. We're in a walled garden." He held the tangle of vines back as Mika opened the door wider and climbed the steps.

Lance emerged behind her.

Once out in the open, Mika studied her surroundings. Like her father had said, the tunnel led into a garden attached to the back of an old school or hotel. The grounds were unkempt, overgrown and appeared rarely used.

Lance crossed to a crooked wooden gate and peered over the top out onto the street beyond.

Mika came to stand beside him. The narrow street on the other side of the gate didn't appear to have any traffic.

Lance lifted the latch and stepped out. "Wait here."

He walked to the end of the street and stopped at the corner. Keeping to the shadows of an old school building, he looked right then left before motioning for them to join him.

Mika and her father left the garden wall and followed Lance to the corner.

"This is as good a place as any for Ketchum to find us." Lance pulled out his cellphone and dropped a pin at their location, sending it to Ketchum via a text message.

A moment later, Ketchum responded.

On our way...ETA ten mikes

"We can wait here in the shadows or back in the garden," Lance said.

Mika studied the busier street from the concealment of the shadowy corner. "I'd rather wait where we can see what's coming."

Mika turned to her father. "Will the priest be all right?"

Her father's mouth pressed into a thin line. "I hope so. He will have enough on his hands repairing the damage to the exterior of the church."

She hugged her father. "I'm just glad you were inside, not in your car."

His arms tightened around her. "Me, too. And I'm glad you weren't close enough to the explosion to be harmed." He frowned. "Guess I'll need a new car when this is all over."

Mika looked up into her father's eyes and gave him a crooked smile. "That's the least of your worries."

He touched her cheek. "Agreed. We have to stay alive long enough to need a new car." With a wink, he turned to the street. "Khaled's people are everywhere, which leads me to believe they're getting through the tunnels from the West Bank again. They'll need to reseal them to stop the flow of suicide bombers from entering Israel."

Minutes later, a non-descript white van slowed to a stop a few yards away.

Lance put out his arm, urging Mika and her father to step back further into the shadows.

A text flashed across Lance's cellphone display, and he called out over his shoulder. "They're here." He waved them forward.

Lance stepped out into the open first, his head swinging left then right as he hurried toward the vehicle.

The side door slid open, and the man Mika recognized as Master Sergeant Ketchum leaned out. "Get in."

Lance helped Mika into the van and then waited for her father to get in before climbing in behind them.

Ketchum slammed the sliding door closed. "Go," he ordered.

The driver pulled away from the curb and blended into traffic.

"Where are we going?" Mika asked.

"To the Israeli airbase nearby. They've set up heightened security around the facility and opened the hangers for temporary housing for the families being targeted by Khaled's men."

"Won't they be watching for people coming and going from the base?" Mika's father asked.

"Probably, but the security forces guarding the base have extended out and searched nearby buildings to make certain there aren't any snipers perched on the roofs or in the windows. They've also set up checkpoints on the roads leading up to the base."

Even with all the precautions they took, Mika knew they couldn't account for everything. Getting into the base would still provide a chokepoint for them and an opportunity for Khaled's men to target them or more family members seeking sanctuary. But they had to go somewhere to be protected until someone could get to Khaled.

As they neared the base, Mika's pulse quickened, and she held her breath, praying they made it through the gauntlet of streets and buildings leading up to the gate.

"You got this, Smoke?" Ketchum asked softly.

"Got it," the driver said. "Going in."

All Mika could see was the road ahead through the two front seats and the windshield. She couldn't tell if someone was waiting atop a building ready to lob grenades or rockets at any vehicle heading onto the base.

Ahead of them, a sedan slowed as it approached the gate.

Smoke slowed the van, waiting for the sedan to clear the gate before closing the distance between the van and the gate guard.

The guard at the gate held up a hand.

Smoke lifted his hands. "Just delivering needed supplies to the temporary residents of the hangers."

The guard conducted a thorough search of the

van's exterior, even using a mirror on a telescoping rod to check for bombs attached to the undercarriage.

The gate guard stepped up to the driver's side window. Leaning into the opening, his eyes narrowed as he surveyed the occupants of the interior.

Mika crawled up to the back of the driver's seat, pulled out her military ID and held it in front of the guard's face. "We're headed for the hangers to meet up with the rest of our team," she said.

After a long narrow-eyed glare, the guard nodded and waved them through.

Once on the base, Mika felt only slightly more secure. If Khaled or his men decided they wanted in, they'd employ whatever means necessary to breach the base security. Then the families and soldiers would all be in danger and an easy target to eliminate all with one strategic bomb. Hell, they had drones that could drop explosives on the hangers and kill everyone inside them.

It was only a matter of time before Hassam figured out where all the families were held. Her heart now thundering against her ribs, Mika felt the need to leap out of the van and search the sky for any sign of a drone. She opened her mouth to tell Smoke to stop the van and let her out.

Before she could say anything, a hand touched hers. She glanced to her right.

Lance curled his fingers around hers and squeezed gently. He met her gaze with a steady one of his own. His gray eyes calmed her with only a glance.

She drew in a deep breath and let it out and, with it, much of the tension building inside.

The van pulled to a stop in front of an airplane hangar.

Major Sharim emerged from the hangar and met the Deltas on the tarmac. "I'm glad you made it. There appears to be a number of Hamas terrorists roaming the streets of Jerusalem."

Ketchum shook the Major's hand. "We hope you were able to evacuate the families to a safe location."

Sharim nodded and waved a hand toward the hanger. "Come see what we have done to ensure the safety of our teams' loved ones."

He led the way through a door into the hangar.

The hum of voices was the first thing that hit Mika as she passed from the bright light of the late afternoon sunshine into the semi-darkness of the hangar. As her vision adjusted, her heart constricted. The empty hangar had been converted into a shelter for the families. Cots had been brought in, folding chairs, blankets and pillows.

"We exercised our disaster preparedness scenario and deployed the items the men, women and children would need to shelter here until such a time as Khaled's men are captured and brought to justice."

The major nodded toward several lines of cafeteria-style tables and chairs where many women and children sat, eating or reading books. "We mobilized a field kitchen and Army cooks to keep people from going hungry and have provisions arriving to sustain them indefinitely."

"Are there more family members out there?" Ketchum asked.

Sharim nodded, his face grave. "We sent out a team of Sayeret Matkal to retrieve them. We have yet to hear from them."

Mika stepped forward. "Are there any plans to go after Khaled?"

Her commanding officer met her gaze with a direct one of his own. "We are in the planning stages."

She lifted her chin. "I wish to be assigned to that mission."

Sharim's lips lifted briefly on the corners, and then straightened into a thin line. "And you will." He glanced around at the Deltas. "If you will... follow me."

Lance walked beside Mika as Sharim led them to the far end of the hangar into a hallway with doors on either side. He stopped in front of the last one, flung open the door and waved them inside.

Mika entered, a surge of relief filling her chest as she recognized the men gathered around a conference table with a map of Israel projected on one of the white walls.

As Mika entered, the men gathered around and hugged her, pounding her back in their enthusiasm. In Hebrew, they congratulated her on making it to the base.

As she looked around the room, noting three missing faces. She met Sharim's gaze. "I saw what happened to Erdan in front of his family home."

The major dipped his head, his eyes shadowed. "As did the entire nation."

"What about Bennett and Landau?" She braced for bad news.

Sharim shook his head. "Landau was hit in a drive-by shooting as he was getting fuel for his vehicle. We haven't heard from Bennett."

Which probably meant the man was lying dead somewhere. Bennett was loyal to the team and would have been there helping plan how they would take out Khaled to end the terror being waged on their families.

"Their families?" Mika asked.

"Bennett's wife and child are in the hangar. Landau's family was the one targeted by a suicide bomber in the market. His wife and mother were killed instantly. His daughter was taken to the hospital. They aren't sure she'll make it."

Mika's hands clenched into fists. "What are we doing to stop this?"

Sharim lifted his chin toward the men gathering around the map again. "We're waiting for intel on

Khaled's whereabouts. Once we have that, we'll launch an attack on him. We suspect he's in the West Bank territory since he was there to torture Yaron. We don't think he would have gone to Gaza. Not when it's so difficult to get in and out."

"What about here in Jerusalem," Ketchum asked. "Are you having any luck catching the terrorists inside the city?"

Sharim nodded. "Some. The police and the Army have teamed to sweep the city to find anyone who doesn't belong. We hope to complete that effort before dark."

One of Sharim's team members keyed on a laptop. The projected image changed, zooming in on a location on the east side of the line dividing Israel and the West Bank.

The computer operator spoke in Hebrew.

Sharim nodded and turned to Mika and the Deltas. "They think they've located him in a small town northeast of Hebron."

"It's too close to Hebron to fly in unnoticed. We were fortunate Yaron had been held in a deserted village. We will not be as lucky this time. He's in a populated area." Sharim snorted. "He's probably surrounded by people hoping we will shoot rockets in their midst and kill civilians so they can prove to the world we are barbaric."

"Are there any border crossings we can drive through?" Ketchum asked.

"Not without announcing ourselves to every Hamas terrorist in the West Bank." Lance studied the satellite map, noting the rugged terrain and the numerous villages along the roads through the country. "We can't rely only on helicopters. They're loud and won't get us close enough before being spotted."

"We can't drive across the border," Sharim said. "The wall and fences were built to keep the Palestinian terrorists out of this side of Israel. On the other hand, it keeps us out of Palestinian-claimed territory."

"What about going cross-country?" Lance asked. "Is it possible to take dirt bikes or all-terrain vehicles, drop them from helicopters in a deserted area and drive them cross-country to get to where Khaled is located?"

Sharim's brow furrowed. "We have motorcycles."

"Can we get a helicopter to drop enough of us to make a difference?" Lance asked.

Ketchum's eyes narrowed. "I might be able to call in a favor. If we can get clearance."

"And if we don't get clearance?" Smoke asked.

Ketchum's lips quirked on the corners. "We conduct a joint training mission with the Israeli Army."

Lance turned to Sharim. "How soon can you get the motorcycles?"

"It might take a day," the Israeli major said. "I'm

not exactly sure where they're stored or even if they're all operational."

"Work on that," Lance said. "We'll arrange for transport."

Ketchum pulled out his cellphone and called his contact.

Mika worked with Sharim, calling everyone she could think of who might know what unit had the motorcycles and where they might be stored. Israel wasn't a huge country, she figured. They should be able to locate the motorcycles before the day was over.

She wasn't sure about the scheme to go cross-country on motorcycles, never having driven in a combat environment or off improved roads. They would be able to go off-road and avoid town centers where people congregated and reported on who passed through town.

They had to move in on Khaled without him being alerted. Otherwise, he'd move to another location, and they'd have to start over in their search for the terrorist.

Mika rubbed her hands over her arms. She'd been so close to losing her father that day. She was ready to do whatever it took to take Khaled down.

CHAPTER 6

Lance and Ketchum worked with the pilots of a Chinook helicopter unit positioned in Turkey. By the time they'd secured a commitment out of Ketchum's higher headquarters, and the unit responsible for the helicopters in Turkey, the sun had set, and stars littered the sky like so much glitter.

Lance and Ketchum caught up with Sharim and Mika.

"We can have the Chinook here tomorrow in the early afternoon."

Sharim nodded. "We've located the motorcycles and have a team of soldiers on their way to their storage location. They'll load the bikes into a truck and, under the cover of night, bring them here. The motorcycles should arrive no later than two o'clock in the afternoon."

"By the time the sun sets tomorrow," Ketchum

said, "we can have motorcycles loaded aboard the choppers and our team ready to go."

They agreed to limit the team to a handful of men…and one woman. Their mission: locate and neutralize Khaled. Once the plan was in place, there was nothing else left to do but wait for the motorcycles and helicopters to appear.

Lance exited the hangar to stand outside in the fresh air, away from the noise of humanity packed into a hanger meant for aircraft, not humans. The hangar smelled of aviation fuel and oil. The people camping out on cots or sleeping bags on the floor deserved to be home in their own beds.

It wasn't safe for any of them to leave the base.

A figure leaned against the wall of the hangar shadowed from the starlight. "You shouldn't be standing out in the open." Mika pushed away from the wall and the shadows. As she neared him, her face was bathed in starlight, giving it a soft indigo blue tint. Her hair had slipped free of the elastic band that had held it back throughout the day. It swung down around her shoulders, softening her appearance.

"I'll take my chances. I feel like this is the first time I've been able to breathe normally today," Lance said.

Mika nodded, lifted her face to the stars, closed her eyes and drew in a deep breath. Her chest rose and fell.

Lance had the feeling she was more exposed at

that moment than just as a target for a drone operator. "You've had a rough day," he commented.

She nodded. "But I'm alive, and my father is, too."

"Things and buildings can be replaced," he said.

"People can't," Mika finished, her voice barely above a whisper.

"True." Lance stepped up beside her and lifted his face to the stars. A cool breeze swept over him. The day had been insane. Thankfully, he'd gone with his gut after watching the news reports that morning. Mika and her father might not be alive now if he hadn't been persistent and found out where she lived. "Why are you outside now? Need air, too?"

She looked away. "I was thinking of sneaking off the base and going back to the church where we met with my father."

Lance frowned. "Seriously? By yourself?" He reached out for her.

She took his hand in hers and gave him half a smile. "Don't worry. I'm not going."

He let go of the breath he hadn't realized he was holding. "Damn right, you're not. And if you did, you better take me. While Khaled is still a threat, I've got your six."

"I like to think I can take care of myself. Today…" She squeezed his hand. "Thanks for being there for my father and me."

He tugged on her hand, drawing her into the circle of his other arm. "I think I died a thousand deaths when your home exploded. You could've been inside."

She chuckled, the sound a bit shaky. "I had a few moments like that today."

"Then why did you want to go back to the church?"

"I was worried about the priest." She looked down at her hand in his, not pulling out of his embrace but leaning into him. "And I wanted to get my things out of the car we left there."

Lance swore softly. "You'd go back there for things?" He stared down into her eyes. "Promise me you won't sneak off into the night. Nothing is that important you'd risk your life for it."

She gave a slight shrug. "I left a photograph of me, my mother and father, along with an album of our lives together in the back seat. I didn't want it to get lost or destroyed. It's possibly all we have left of her. My father loved my mother deeply."

"Oh, baby." Lance dropped her hand and pulled her into both arms, crushing her to him. "I get it. But your father would rather have you alive for the future than have old photos of the past."

She nodded, pressing her cheek against his chest. "It's just that he loved my mother, and all he had left of her were the photos."

"How long has it been since she died?" he asked, smoothing a hand over her silky dark hair.

"Twenty-three years," she whispered, her fingers curling into his chest.

"That's a long time." He cupped the back of her head in his palm. "Could losing the photos be a good thing for him?"

She frowned and looked up at him, her eyes so dark in the shadows. "What do you mean?"

"Maybe losing the photos will force him to let go of his memory of her." Lance held up his hands. "Not forget, but let go enough to get on with life. Is it right for a man to grieve for a woman for the rest of his life?"

Mika's frown deepened. "You think my father will forget my mother if he loses a few photographs? He loved her so deeply, he almost didn't want to live after she died." She shook her head. "Have you ever been in love?" A single dark brow rose.

Lance stared down into her dark eyes, mesmerized by the fierce passion in them. He wanted to reach out, capture her face and kiss her full, sexy lips until she couldn't stand, much less toss words at him like a challenge.

Her chin lifted high. "I don't mean pathetically casual love. What I'm talking about is deep love. The kind of love where you can't imagine life without that one person beside you?"

His eyebrows pulled together over his nose. "No." His arms tightened around her as he asked, "Have you?"

She didn't push away from him or attempt to step out of his embrace. "Well, I've never been in a relationship where I've felt that way. But I've watched my father as he grieved for my mother all these years. He would buy flowers to put on her grave every birthday and anniversary and again on the day marking her death. Images of them together hung in the living room and his bedroom. Yeah, he loved her more than time itself, considering he hasn't dated or allowed himself to date or fall in love again."

His brow twisted, and he gave her a wry smile. "Is that healthy?"

Mika stared out into the night and sighed. "I don't know. I've thought for a long time he should find someone, a companion, a lover. He deserves to be happy again. Falling in love again wouldn't be dishonoring my mother. I have to believe she would have wanted him to be happy, even if it was without her."

"Everyone deserves a little happiness." Lance cupped her cheek and brushed a thumb over her lips. "What about you? Are you happy, or are you too worried about your father's happiness to go after your own?"

Her body stilled. She looked up into his eyes, her own inky pools in the shadows. "I never really thought about it. I worked hard to make it as a Sayeret Matkal."

"I get that. I've worked hard, too." Lance's lips

quirked. For him, Delta Force had been a personal goal as well as a team effort. "I made it into the elite force, and I put everything into successful missions for my country and my brothers in arms."

"Same," she said.

He nodded. "But lately, I've felt like something is missing."

"You have?" Her brow furrowed.

"I have." His thumb brushed across her lips again. They were so soft. So tempting. He bent to touch her lips with his. Gentle, at first. A soft feathery kiss. He was almost afraid to spook her or make her mad. But, damn, he wanted the kiss so much he was willing to risk being slapped in the face or worse.

That simple brush of his mouth to hers sent sparks firing through his veins, setting off a chain reaction throughout his body, culminating in a tightened groin.

When he started to lift his head to gauge her reaction, he was surprised when her hands reached up to lace behind the back of his neck.

Mika brought his mouth back to hers, crushing him to her.

He engulfed her in his arms, pressing her body to his, reveling in her warmth and delicious curves. Soft in all the usual places, she was tightly packed, her muscles strong and toned.

For a long moment, time stood still, the plight of their circumstances fading into the background, and they could've been anywhere, and he wouldn't have noticed anything but the woman in his arms.

He traced the seam of her lips with the tip of his tongue.

Immediately, she opened to him.

When her teeth parted, he dove in, sliding his tongue along the length of hers, loving the warmth, wetness and sensuality in that one kiss. It went on forever yet ended far too soon.

As he lifted his head to breathe, a moan slid up Lance's throat. He leaned his head back, drew in a deep breath and let it out slowly. "I've wanted to do that since you climbed into the helicopter next to me."

She shook her head. "Seriously? I wore combat gear and carried a high-powered rifle. I could have been there to kill you."

"And you were completely badass and fierce." He cupped her cheek again.

"Most men are intimidated by women in the military," she said, staring up into his eyes.

"I'm not most men. I like a woman who can hold her own in a conversation as well as on the battlefield. My mother was a strong woman. I admired her for that. And for the way she loved my father—unconditionally and with all of her heart."

"Sounds like you had a good childhood." She gave a short, hard laugh. "You know about my father and mother. I know very little about you."

"I was born in Texas; my father and mother met in the Army. They retired when I was a teen and settled in Copperas Cove, a little town outside of Fort Hood…also in Texas. I was a military brat all that time, and I knew I'd join the Army as soon as I graduated high school. It was in my blood. My parents set the example of dedication to their country as well as to their family."

"Siblings?" she asked.

"A brother and a sister."

"You were the oldest?"

He nodded.

"Did they join the military like you?"

He grinned. "My sister did. My brother chose to go into law enforcement. He's a member of the Texas Rangers."

"And your sister? Where is she now?"

He grinned. "Stationed in Korea. So, you see? I'm not at all intimidated by strong women. I'm proud of them and all they've accomplished."

"You are the exception," she said, her mouth firming into a straight line. "I have to prove myself every day, or the men of my unit will think I am weak. I could never fall in love. They would consider me too soft, unable to fight at their sides."

"And if they were to fall in love?"

"They would still fight fiercely. That's what men do." She snorted softly.

"My mother was every bit as fierce as my father. My sister, too."

She smiled up at him. "You are the exception. And I don't have to live and fight beside you every day." Mika took a step backward. "And we should get some rest. Tomorrow will be a long day."

The distance she put between them seemed greater than the two feet it actually was.

Lance wanted to pull her back into his arms and kiss her again. Once was not nearly enough. That kiss had only awakened in him the need to touch her again. The reality of their situation was hardly conducive to furthering contact or deepening a relationship.

Mika was a member of the IDF, her life in Israel. Lance was an American with a life slated for combat and dangerous missions all over the world. The U.S. Army owned him for the duration of his current enlistment, which didn't end for another year, and he had no plans to get out until he hit twenty years.

Anything he might have with Mika would be fleeting, lasting only the duration of this mission. Their paths would never cross again after he left Israel.

His chest tightened. He wanted their paths to cross. He wanted more than this mission to spend time with her. He had to think of something, some way…

Lance reached for her hand and tugged her gently.

She didn't resist when he pulled her back into his arms. "I'm glad we met," he said before his mouth descended to claim hers in a kiss so gentle it made him long for a lifetime of them. When he raised his head, he pushed aside his own wants and needs. "Come on. Let's find a place to rest. Like you said, tomorrow will be a long day."

She let him take her hand and lead her back into the hangar and to the offices in the rear, where several of her team members and the Deltas had stretched out on sleeping bags to get some much-needed sleep. Her father lay near the door, asleep on his side, his head resting on his arm.

Lance found a couple of sleeping bags in a corner and tossed one to Mika.

He unrolled his bag in an empty space at the end of a long conference table.

Mika laid hers out beside his and sank onto it.

Lance liked that she chose to sleep beside him. It wasn't as if anything would happen in a room crowded with others. But knowing she preferred to be close to him made his heart swell. If there was any way he could make something last between them...

He sighed and laid down beside her.

A moment later, she reached for his hand.

In the dark, on the hard floor, threatened by a

Hamas terrorist, with a future where massive distances would separate them, they lay side by side, holding hands.

For that moment, Lance knew it had to be enough.

But it wasn't.

M<small>IKA LAY</small> awake for a long time, her hand in Lance's, her heart beating fast, her thoughts jumbled. How could she think about anything but the coming mission to find and eliminate Khaled Aziz? So many lives depended on a successful outcome.

And yet, she lay beside a man she hadn't known long, an American who would be leaving to go back to the States when the mission was over in a short amount of time. And she was holding his hand, loving the strength of his fingers wrapped around hers.

She knew she didn't need a man in her life. But it felt good to kiss the American, to lie next to him, holding his hand. The problem she had was that she wanted so much more than just to hold his hand.

She wanted to be somewhere they could be alone. After the two kisses they'd shared, her thoughts had gone from the mission to what it would feel like to lie in a bed with this man…naked.

Holding his hand, lying beside him, her body

burned for so much more. Never in her life had she felt this strong of an attraction to a man. No, she wasn't a virgin. She'd had sex. But those encounters had been different. She hadn't felt any desire to continue those relationships afterward. She'd felt little regret when she'd walked away.

Now, without having made love or done much more than kiss, her heart ached, her gut was tight and her core was so hot she could barely lie still and definitely couldn't sleep.

For a long time, she lay awake, imagining Lance's fingers—the ones holding hers—running over her naked skin, from her breasts down to the juncture of her thighs and…and…

She swallowed a moan, let go of his hand and turned onto her side, facing away from him. Maybe lying next to him was a mistake. She would never get the rest she needed. Not when she was imagining him making love to her, his hands and mouth touching every part of her body. And she wanted to explore every inch of his. What was wrong with her? He was just a man.

A powerful and virile man who wasn't the least daunted by her career choice.

She lay for a long time, willing herself to sleep. After her tenth sigh, she was ready to get up and give up on rest.

Lance's arm wrapped around her and pulled her

back up against his front. He spooned her against his body, his arm holding her close. He was warm, solid and smelled so good. She didn't fight him. Instead, she leaned back into his embrace.

Yes. This was where she wanted to be. No. They weren't making love. But it was the next best thing.

Mika relaxed, breathed deeply and reveled in his strength and acceptance. He wasn't afraid of her or intimidated by her strength. She had nothing to prove to him. That felt good. It was freeing and addictive. She could get used to being with such a man. This man.

Ah, but who was she fooling? They could never be together as long as each was in their current positions in their respective military forces.

An overwhelming sadness washed over her, tamping down the heat of desire. She and Lance had no future together, not that he was asking, or she was considering it.

They would soon have an ocean between them. Yes, there was such a thing as long-distance relationships. But an ocean away? Even that was too much to ask of anyone.

Nestling against the American, she quit thinking about the negatives of an empty future and focused on the positives of the present. His arms were around her. His body was pressed to hers, and she was warm and safe. Tomorrow would come all too soon.

She pulled Lance's arm close, resting it beneath her breast, not caring what her teammates would say or think. As she drifted into a troubled sleep, her last thought was of how good it felt to be in this tall, handsome American's arms.

CHAPTER 7

LANCE WOKE before Mika and lay in the dark for a long while, holding the woman in his arms, inhaling the clean, fresh scent of her hair. He knew she'd catch all kinds of grief from her teammates if they found her cuddling with the American, but he didn't want to let go. So, he held her a bit longer until the rustle of movement alerted him to others in the room, waking to the early morning gray of dawn.

Careful not to wake her, Lance slipped his arm from around her and rolled away, already missing the warmth and softness of her curves pressed against his length. He needed the time away from her body to get his own in check. His morning erection pressed hard against the zipper of his trousers.

For the next few minutes, he thought about motorcycles and the mission ahead to relieve the tension in his groin. When he had himself under control, he got up and left the conference room to search for a bathroom and a cup of coffee, in that order.

A coffee machine had been set up in the hangar breakroom and already had a pot steaming on the burner. He found a paper cup and poured himself some of the fragrant brew.

As he sipped the hot liquid, his cellphone vibrated in his back pocket.

He pulled it out, wondering who would be calling so early.

When he recognized Rucker's name on the screen, he answered quickly. "Hey, Rucker. What's the word?"

"Just landed in Ankara, Turkey. Should be in Jerusalem in a couple of hours. You haven't started the party without us, have you?"

Lance chuckled. "Wouldn't dare. You're bringing the beer, right?"

"Beer...right." Rucker laughed. "You can count on it."

"Who'd you get to come?" Lance asked.

"The whole team."

"With Uncle Sam's blessing?"

Rucker hesitated. "Sort of."

"What do you mean sort of?"

"It's in the works, but we didn't want to wait for the official word. We found a Space Available military plane headed your way and got on it."

Lance hoped the approval to participate would come before they headed into Palestinian territory. If not...that going rogue thing was happening.

"What's the plan?" Rucker asked.

Weight lifted from Lance's shoulders with his teammate's acceptance of a mission that might not be condoned by the powers that be in Washington. His team had his back, no matter what. "We'll fill you in when you get here. I'll send a GPS pin of our location."

"Roger. See ya in a few."

As the call ended, Lance turned and glanced across the room at the door. His pulse quickened, and the day seemed to grow brighter.

Mika stood there, her sleek black hair slipping out of her ponytail and her face flushed with sleep. "Coffee?"

He poured her a cup and met her halfway across the room.

She wrapped her hands around the warm cup, closed her eyes and inhaled the steamy scent before taking a tentative sip. "Ah. I needed that."

The sleepy, sexy way she looked had Lance hot in all the wrong places, again. He swallowed hard before asking, "Sleep any?"

Mika nodded. "Better than I would have expected on a hard floor." Her gaze met his. "Thanks. What about you?"

He nodded. "I got enough." The few hours he'd

managed were more than some nights before a mission.

Ketchum and Sharim joined them in the breakroom in search of coffee.

"My teammates from Fort Hood are on their way," Lance said. "They should be here in a few hours."

"How are they getting here?" Sharim asked.

"Black Hawk," Lance said.

Sharim dipped his head. "How many men?"

"Seven."

Ketchum nodded. "Good. We could use backup should the mission go south."

Lance's eyes narrowed. "They're going to want to be with us."

"We won't have enough motorcycles for everyone," Sharim said.

"True," Ketchum said. "And we can't take everyone in without making it obvious we're there."

"Then they can be on standby until we need them," Lance said. "We don't know what we're getting into or how bad it might be. They're coming to help. Hopefully, we won't need their help, but it doesn't hurt to have a backup plan."

"The motorcycles will be here within a couple of hours," Sharim said. "We'll need to familiarize ourselves on their use before we load them into the helicopters and tie them down."

"In the meantime, we need to get an update from our intelligence sources," Sharim said.

"We have to locate our target before we can go anywhere."

Coffees in hand, they left the breakroom and hurried down the hallway to the conference room.

Everyone who'd camped out in the room had gotten up, rolled and stowed their sleeping bags in a stack against the wall and out of the way.

A computer had been set up on the table, connected to a projector. A map of Israel spread out across the white wall of the conference room.

Lance studied the town names inside the dotted lines separating the West Bank from the rest of Israel. A border wall had been erected to keep suicide bombers from easily crossing over to terrorize innocents in marketplaces or taking out government targets. So far, the walls had cut violence significantly. But all bets would be off once they crossed into Palestinian territory.

Sharim and Ketchum pulled out their cellphones and touched bases with their respective intelligence people and the air transportation they would need to get the motorcycles and men into the West Bank to capture or kill Khaled.

Lance and Mika stood by, waiting to hear what they were hearing.

Smoke, Ice and Gonzo joined them in the conference room, along with other members of Sharim's team.

Once Ketchum and Sharim completed their calls, everyone took a seat at that table.

Ketchum nodded to Sharim, who started.

"Our people inside the West Bank have located Khaled in a small town south of Hebron. They said he is surrounded by at least thirty Hamas soldiers. It was said he chose that location due to its proximity to Gaza. He could quickly get into Gaza and hide in the streets or wage his war from there by shooting rockets into Israel."

"What's the status of rounding up Khaled's people here on the streets of Jerusalem?" Ketchum asked.

"Four people were apprehended between yesterday and this morning. One of them had a vest filled with explosives. Fortunately, his detonator malfunctioned; otherwise, the police who took him into custody would not have lived to tell about it. The other three had hand-held grenades in their pockets. Two of the three were captured before they could pull the pins. The third pulled the pin and threw the grenade, but the police officer he'd thrown it at was once a star soccer player. He kicked the grenade back at the thrower and ducked around the corner of a building as the grenade exploded. He escaped injury. The terrorist did not. He was taken to the hospital for his injuries. Once he is treated, he will be moved to jail to await a court hearing to decide his fate."

"That's four," Mika said. "We still have no idea of how many terrorists Khaled sent into Jerusalem. Until he's captured or killed, he will continue to terrorize our families."

The combined American and Israeli team worked together to develop a plan of attack. They would fly around the wall separating the Palestinian-held territory from the rest of Israel and set down in a field south of the town where Khaled was hiding. They'd travel by road or cross country on motorcycles, stopping short of the town to go in on foot under cover of night. Their intel had the exact building their target could be found in and would maintain a vigilant watch to ensure he didn't leave before the team arrived to take him.

Once they had Khaled, they'd call in a helicopter pickup at an extraction point just south of the small town.

The team went over the plan again, breaking only when food was brought in. They sat around the conference table eating and discussing the mission, sports and politics around the world. The two teams from different countries would mesh as well on this mission as it had on the previous one that had brought Yaron out alive. They all agreed that the Deputy Minister's actions had been rash and had cost them more grief than if one of their team had been killed during the extraction.

Those whose families were safely inside the hangar were angry for those who'd lost their families and their lives in the attacks in Jerusalem.

Lance could only imagine how he'd feel if someone went after his loved ones and killed them in retribution for his actions. He worried that Khaled would find his way across the ocean and harm his parents, brother or sister. Concerned about their safety, even on American soil, he stepped out of the hangar to call his father.

"Lance, I thought you were deployed?" his father answered.

"I am. I don't have much time; I just wanted to warn you and the rest of the family that we angered a Hamas terrorist. He's promised to harm the families of those involved in a mission here. If he finds a way to get his people across the ocean, or activate sleeper cells in the U.S., you all might be in trouble."

"Got it. I'll notify your brother and sister to keep their eyes open for trouble. Your mother and I are headed out for a cross-country RV trip. I don't have an itinerary. We're going to drive until we feel like stopping. I doubt anyone will find us without working hard at it. In the meantime, we'll be available by cellphone in case you or your siblings need us."

A grin formed on Lance's face. "Glad you and Mom are enjoying your motorhome and retirement. You've worked hard. You deserve some fun."

"Yeah, and if I don't get moving, your mother will leave without me. Love you, son. Stay safe and come home in one piece."

"Yes, sir. Love you and Mom. Be safe on the road."

"Roger," his father said.

Lance ended the call, turned and found Mika standing behind him.

"Warning your family?" she asked.

He nodded. "I don't think anything will happen to them in the States," he said. "Still, it doesn't hurt to warn them."

"Agreed." Mika nodded toward a truck pulling up to the hangar. "I came out to tell you our motorcycles have arrived."

"Good. I want to familiarize myself before we hit the road on them." He tilted his head. "How much riding have you done?"

She shrugged. "I'm sure not as much as you have. But my father taught me how when I was thirteen. I didn't forget. We still have the motorcycle." Her lips pressed into a thin line. "Well, up until yesterday, we had it. I'm not sure what, if anything, survived the attack on my father's home."

"You'll have time to go through the debris after we make the world a safer place without Khaled planning terror attacks against your families and teammates."

She nodded. "Let's go see what we have." Mika led the way to the truck, where the members of their teams gathered around to help unload the motorcycles, one at a time.

A fuel truck arrived to fill their tanks, and soon, the tarmac filled with motorcycles and riders, testing the engines, brakes and tires.

Lance felt completely at home on the cycle. He'd driven a similar one back in Texas. These had been painted either in camouflage or desert tan or olive drab green. No frills, no shiny mufflers and no wild colors like some of those he'd seen on the dirt bike track back home. After fueling up and making sure the bikes would perform the functions they needed, they parked them beside the hangar where they would wait for the Chinook helicopters that would be loaded with men and equipment needed to go into enemy territory and then come back out.

Lance was happy to see Mika driving her motorcycle with precision and efficiency. He'd been afraid she might not be as confident as she'd indicated.

As Mika parked her bike, a U.S. Black Hawk helicopter arrived on the tarmac near the hangar. The men of his Delta Force team leaped out and strode toward him and the others.

Glad to see their familiar faces, Lance hurried out

to greet them. He was met with back-pounding hugs and warm handshakes, smiles and laughter.

These men were his brothers, his family. He had to admit; he was glad they were there. They'd been on enough missions together that they could think ahead and anticipate each other's actions and responses to situations. He didn't have that with the current Deltas, though they'd worked together fine on the previous mission. They all had the best interests of each other and their country at heart. They would do the right things and have each other's backs.

The team met in the conference room and went over what would happen.

"We can't take everyone in, and we don't have enough motorcycles for the rest of your team, Ketchum said. "But we could use the guns on the Black Hawk to provide protection for the Chinooks as they land and offload the riders who will go after Khaled."

Rucker nodded. "We're there in case you run into trouble."

"Now, all we have to do is wait for sunset," Sharim said. "We will leave as daylight dims on the horizon. I suggest we rest until then."

Ha. Like that was going to happen. The last thing Lance could imagine doing was lying down and taking a power nap for the next three hours. Already, his mind had taken him to the open field where they would land, offload the motorcycles and take off in search of Khaled.

He prayed the intelligence operative in Palestine was completely accurate in determining where Khaled was holed up. With Khaled hiding in a village full of people, there could be multiple instances of collateral damage. Meaning, they could hurt or kill innocent civilians in the process of finding and neutralizing the terrorist, Khaled. Yaron had already made it bad enough by bombing Khaled's home with his wife and children inside.

Lance could hardly blame Khaled for fighting back and terrorizing the families of the Sayeret Matkal team that had been instrumental in freeing Yaron. He'd be after blood as well if someone went after the people he loved.

His thoughts strayed to Mika. He'd hate for her or other members of his family to be killed because of some diplomat's poor decision, leading to the deaths of women and children. Anger burned at Yaron's actions. And from the reactions of the other Israeli special forces guys, they were equally mad about what their government had allowed. Now, they had to protect their own families at the same time as they had to go after the man giving the orders.

Leaving his family behind for someone else to protect went against the grain for Lance. Then again, who else had the specialized skills necessary to seek out and destroy Khaled to end the terror?

Rucker found Lance after the briefing, a smirk curving the corners of his lips. "Hack, huh?"

He chuckled at the use of the nickname the other Delta team had come up with for him. "Yeah."

"Like the new callsign," Tank said. "Better than some."

Blade laughed. "Like Shithead?"

"Much better." Lance smiled at the usual joking his team did before a mission. It helped calm their nerves and keep things light when it was about to get serious.

"You okay with all of this?" Rucker tipped his head toward the other group of Delta Force operators.

Lance nodded. "The Deltas we went in with initially are highly trained. They know their stuff. Ketchum has more years of service than you or I. His team has been together for quite some time."

"I get that. You, however, haven't been with them for that long. Do you want to stay back with us and let the IDF handle finding and neutralizing Khaled?"

Lance's gaze sought out Mika's. She stepped up beside him and cocked an eyebrow, indicating she'd overheard the conversation.

He could no more let Mika go alone into a Palestinian-held area than he could let his sister, brother or parents. She meant something to him. How that had happened in such a short amount of time, he was not entirely sure. Watching her in action, knowing her capabilities and determination had made him want to know more about this remarkable woman who wouldn't let a little thing like her gender hold her back from helping her country. She knew her mind, knew her strengths and used them to their best advantage.

He couldn't guarantee a future with Mika, but he sure as hell would be with her on this mission. After that… Well, he'd figure out some way to get to see her again.

The sun sank low on the horizon.

"If we're going to do this, let's get this show on the road," Ketchum spoke loud enough every member of the combined team could hear.

They checked their weapons, tightened buckles on their body armor and patted their ammo magazines reassuringly. After a final communications check with their radio headsets, the motorcycle team climbed aboard the Chinooks.

Lance felt strange loading onto a different aircraft than the rest of his team. At the same time, he felt right about being with the combined IDF and Delta team. He'd bonded with them over the threat to their families from the Hamas leader who'd ordered hits on them.

In the encroaching darkness, he slid onto the seat beside Mika. He curled his fingers around hers and then tucked their clasped hands between where their legs touched. The motorcycles were strapped to the floor between the benches where the team sat for the duration of the flight. Being behind enemy lines wasn't new for Lance. Going into a battle on a motorcycle was a new experience. He hoped this tactic would work. They needed to get in, find Khaled and get the hell out…preferably alive.

CHAPTER 8

Mika sat beside Lance on the flight, her hand in his, out of sight of the others. Being the only female on the team made her a target of scrutiny. Holding hands with a member of the team would be frowned upon. Usually, she'd avoid any public displays of affection. She'd fought hard to be considered worthy of her position in the Sayeret Matkal. Probably harder than most of the men on the team. Once they made it through the training, they were accepted.

Not Mika. She had to constantly prove herself, or they'd see her as weak. So, holding hands with a member of an attack team was a big deal. After what they'd been through that day, Mika didn't care if someone caught her holding hands with the American. If anyone commented, she'd pound him into the ground to prove herself, yet again.

Light faded from the sky as they lifted off the

tarmac of the military airfield and rose above the city of Jerusalem. Streetlights blinked on below, shining over the ancient structures and the modern buildings. This holy city had been her home for all her life. Even when she'd been stationed at other locations in the country, she knew she could always come home to her father's house. She would always have a place here.

Until Khaled had her home destroyed. Now, as she stared down at the city, growing smaller by the minute, the realization that the house she'd grown up in was gone hit her hard. She had to remind herself that her losses could have been worse. Her father could have been in that house or his car when they exploded. Her father had dedicated his life to his country by joining the military. He'd continued his service as a private contractor, working with the government.

He deserved to retire and live the rest of his life in peace.

Mika thought of the vacation Lance had planned on the lake near Fort Hood. Her father liked fishing. He would enjoy sitting on a dock, in a boat or standing on the bank, dipping his hook in the water. When this mission was over, she'd take that vacation she'd planned. She would go to the U.S. and visit the hometown her mother had grown up in. Maybe she'd ask Lance about the cabin on the lake. She could stay in a place like that and throw a line in the water.

Now that her father's home had been destroyed, he might consider going with her.

Her service anniversary was coming up. That date gave her the opportunity to choose a different life. She'd never considered anything other than the Sayeret Matkal life. Having worked so hard to get into the elite, usually all-male special forces unit, she figured it was a career commitment she'd continue in throughout her military career.

Her father had been a military man and had raised his only daughter, with the help of nannies and other military families who'd stepped in when he'd deployed to other parts of the world.

Mika hadn't considered having children. Being pregnant, giving birth weren't things the members of the elite special forces did. She'd have to give up the position she'd fought so hard to attain and retain. She couldn't go into a hostile environment pregnant. Her lips quirked at the mental image of her with a big belly, body armor, helmet and carrying her rifle.

"What's so funny?" Lance asked.

Her cheeks heated. "Nothing."

The thought of being pregnant, carrying a child inside her, had never occurred to her until she'd met Lance.

Why now?

They were about to go into hostile territory and fight a particularly evil terrorist, known for torturing his victims and using them as examples for other

Islamist extremists to follow. He'd urged his followers to decapitate the infidel Jews to drive them from the Holy Land. He would be surrounded by his men, not an easy target to extract alive.

Her jaw tightened. She wasn't concerned about bringing the man out alive. His path had been one of death and destruction, killing innocents, with no regard for human lives other than his own.

Then again, it would be far better to kill Khaled rather than risk the chance of his escaping to continue his reign of terror.

"Now, you're frowning," Lance squeezed her hand. "We're going to be all right."

Mika nodded. "Just thinking of all the evil for which Khaled has been responsible."

"Is that how you get into the mission mindset?"

"Sometimes. And sometimes, I think of other things."

"For instance?"

"Like fishing, and how I would like to visit this lake of yours in Texas." She smiled. "It sounds peaceful."

"Is that what you were thinking when you smiled earlier?" he asked.

Her cheeks heated again. "Yes," she lied. There was no way she'd tell him she was thinking of her belly being big with a baby inside. Why she'd even thought about being pregnant had nothing to do with having met Lance. Another lie. This time to herself.

What would it be like to be pregnant with the American's baby? What would it be like to be a mother? She barely knew that role, having been raised by her father. Sure, the nannies and the mothers who'd taken her in during her father's deployments had been warm, nurturing and loving. But she hadn't had that influence consistently since her mother had passed away. Would she be a good mother? Would she be willing to sacrifice all she'd worked so hard to achieve to be home with a child?

Her vague memories of her sweet mother were of being cuddled and kissed. Of having her hair brushed gently and being read to and sung to when she went to bed at night. Could she do those things as well as her mother had?

Her father had done his best to be there at night when he could. He'd read to her, but he'd never sung lullabies. Instead, he'd taken her fishing and taught her self-dense and how to shoot a gun. He'd probably considered those activities much better use of his and her time. She would always be able to protect herself. And if she was lost in the wild, she could eat fish to survive.

Lance's fingers gently squeezed around hers. "You know, I can take you fishing when you come to the States. I'd like that."

She returned the pressure on her hand with a squeeze of her own. "I'd like that, too."

For the rest of the flight, she forced herself to focus on the task at hand.

As they neared their drop zone, the team rose and positioned themselves beside their respective motorcycles, waiting for the cue to release the buckles that held the bikes in place.

The chopper landed with a gentle bump.

Mika leaned down and unbuckled the straps holding her motorcycle in place. She mounted the bike and started the engine.

By the time the back door dropped, the team was ready.

As soon as the ramp touched the ground, the riders closest to the door shot out, weapons looped over their shoulders.

Mika and Lance were the last out the door.

Ketchum and Sharim took the lead, their GPS devices guiding the string of cyclists through the countryside toward their destination.

The Chinooks would fly back across the barrier between the West Bank and the rest of Israel to wait for a call to pick up the team. The Black Hawk would wait on the other side of the border and wait for word from the team on motorcycles. If the team ran into trouble, others could be there in minutes to provide air support or additional troops on the ground.

They'd planned a route that would take them northwest along roads that would not be heavy with traffic. When they approached towns, they would go off-road to bypass them. They drove with their lights off, relying on starlight to guide them. A clear sky made that possible with a blanket of stars shining brightly.

They didn't have far to go. The time it would take to get from the drop zone to the outskirts of the small town where Khaled was hiding should only take them twenty minutes, depending on any resistance they might encounter.

For the first ten minutes, they followed a road.

Ahead, the lead motorcycles left the pavement and traveled off-road, paralleling the road, far enough away they wouldn't be seen by anyone on the main road. They bypassed a small town and converged on the road again after they'd cleared the last building.

Not long afterward, the lead bikers swerved off the road and down into a ravine, slowing until they were completely stopped.

The convoy of bikes followed suit. Mika came to a stop. Lance brought up the rear, coming to a halt two meters behind her.

They weren't far from a road juncture and could see the headlights of vehicles coming from the east, heading west along the road they'd been on.

From what Mika could see, they were trucks. In the backs of the trucks were men seated on the sides of the beds. Each carried a rifle.

Her pulse quickened. They were heading for the small town where Khaled was located.

This could be bad. They could be reinforcements there to protect the Hamas leader.

Even though it was late at night, they'd be awake and, if attacked, prepared to defend.

Their mission could just have gotten harder.

They waited for the trucks to pass. Once they were out of sight, the lead motorcycles reclaimed the paved road and followed at a safe distance.

"We need to get to where we're going right behind the guys who passed us," Sharim said into Mika's headset. "While they're still settling in and confused."

Which meant that once they left their motorcycles, they had to hurry into the town on foot, no time to reconnoiter.

Mika fell in behind the others, with Lance covering her rear.

Shortly after they resumed their ride, the lead motorcycles left the road again.

Ahead, lights shone from the small town. Their destination.

Adrenaline pushed through her veins. She would be glad to dismount and go the rest of the way on foot. Riding a motorcycle wasn't conducive to firing one's weapon. They were, however, good for getting away quickly. In that respect, she didn't look forward to leaving them behind.

After bumping along on uneven terrain, doing her

best to avoid large rocks, small bushes and an occasional tree, Mika was glad to see they were getting closer to the town. Close enough to leave their motorcycles as soon as Ketchum and Sharim found a good place to stage them for their return to a reasonable position for extraction.

Moments later, the riders in front of her slowed to a stop, shut off the engines and dismounted.

"We push our bikes from here," Ketchum said. "The closer we can get in silence, the better. But spread out. We don't want Khaled's men to take us out with one well-placed grenade."

Again, he and Sharim led the way. Mika and Lance fanned out to the far west of the others.

When they reached the outskirts of the small town, Sharim said, "Find a place to hide your motorcycle and remember where it is. We'll need them on the way out."

Mika eased up to the back of a stone, stick and mud wall and laid her bike on its side in the shadows. She pulled her knife from its sheath around her thigh, cut a branch from a nearby bush and laid it on top of the motorcycle.

All the while, she kept her eye on Lance doing the same near the far end of the same walled dwelling.

Cutting a branch from a tree, she carried it over to where Lance stood beside his motorcycle and laid the branch across the vehicle.

She lifted her rifle strap over her head and brought her weapon down into the ready position.

Lance did the same, moving toward the others.

"Smoke and Ice, circle the perimeter of town to the west," Ketchum said. Two other Deltas were sent to secure the south entrance to town. "Gonzo and Hack, you're with me when we go in."

Sharim called out in Hebrew to the Sayeret Matkal team to secure the east and north. They were to spread out and report what they found in the way of sentries and other Hamas fighters.

Mika didn't like that the Americans would be going one way and IDF soldiers the other. She'd hoped she would be able to go where Lance went and cover his back.

"Mika Blue," Sharim added, "you're to go with Hack. As you did in the Yaron extraction, you will take the lead once we have located Khaled. You two will follow Ketchum, Gonzo and me into the town while the others secure the perimeter."

Relief washed over Mika. She nodded toward her team leader and remained close to Lance as they followed Sharim and Ketchum through the narrow streets.

Engine noises and shouts sounded ahead at the heart of the little town.

At the next street corner, Ketchum hunkered down, raised his weapon to his shoulder and eased around the corner.

He raised his left hand and motioned Sharim and Gonzo forward.

Sharim slipped up to where Ketchum knelt at the corner then, crouching low, disappeared. Gonzo did the same.

A moment later, Ketchum followed,

Mika ran quietly to the position Ketchum had held and covered for Lance, who slipped around the corner to find another spot in the shadows.

The five soldiers leap-frogged until they reached a point where they were close enough to see where the trucks were congregated. Men with guns slung over their shoulders moved about, unloading boxes and carrying them into a larger building surrounded by a six-foot wall.

"Gonzo," Ketchum whispered. "You know what to do."

Gonzo nodded, backed away from his position and slipped into the shadows behind them.

Two minutes later, Gonzo reported, "Have a bird's eye view from the top of the building in front of you."

"Smoke and Ice in position inside the west end of town," Smoke said. "Took out one sentry on the road leading in. West entrance secured. No other guards between the north and south."

"Good," Ketchum said. "Bring it in. We'll need all the firepower we can get."

Sharim's men reported having taken out the

sentries on the east and north roads leading into town. He ordered his guys to move closer.

It was time to move in before Khaled realized his perimeter guards had been removed and he alerted the rest of his men.

"Let's do this," Ketchum whispered.

"Gotcha covered," Gonzo assured him from his position overlooking the front of the walled compound Khaled occupied.

Ketchum and Sharim backed away from the town center and circled to the back of the large building the Hamas terrorists were carrying supplies into.

Lance and Mika followed.

An armed guard was positioned at each of the back corners. They stood at the ready but talking to each other in Arabic.

"The guards are exchanging bets on an upcoming football game," Sharim said softly into Mika's headset.

"Lance, take the guard on the east corner," Ketchum said. "I'll take the other. Moving into position."

Another moment later, Ketchum said, "On three."

Lance raised his rifle with the silencer in place and aimed at the man.

"One…" Ketchum whispered, "two…three."

Lance squeezed the trigger. A soft *poomph* sound escaped the barrel of his weapon. The east sentry dropped at the same time the man on the other corner did.

Sharim and Ketchum rushed to the base of the wall, grabbed the dead sentry by the ankles and pulled him into the brush.

Sharim beat Ketchum back to the wall, bent and cupped his hands.

Ketchum raced after Sharim, stepped into his cupped hands and launched himself at the top of the wall.

After Mika and Lance hid their guy in the brush, Mika sprinted past Lance, knelt at the base of the wall and offered her back, knowing it was the most reliable way she could offer the big Delta a boost up the wall.

When Lance hesitated, Mika urged. "Just do it."

Lance ran toward her and planted his boot in the center of her back.

As he pushed down, she raised up.

He made it to the top of the wall and flung his leg over.

For a moment, Lance and Ketchum lay still, their gazes turned toward the inner sanctum of the walled complex.

As one, they turned back to the two on the ground.

Ketchum grasped Sharim's hand at the same time Lance reached for Mika's.

With Lance's help, Mika pulled herself up to

straddle the wall. As soon as all four were on top, they laid flat against the brick and mud surface to blend into the wall should anyone happen to look back.

The very back of the building had one door at the center. It was closed and didn't have a sentry standing guard over it.

"Going down to scout the east side," Sharim whispered as he slid over the side and quietly dropped to his feet. He disappeared around the side of the building.

"I'll take the opposite side," Lance said and slipped to the ground inside the wall.

From her position on top of the wall, Mika followed Lance's progress until he disappeared around another corner.

"We have company," Sharim whispered.

Mika pulled her gaze from Lance. The back door of the building opened. Two men exited. One turned left, the other went right.

Mika reached for her knife and waited, praying the man headed her way didn't see her. She held her breath, afraid she might make a sound and give herself and the team away.

The sentry called out to his counterpart just as Sharim leaped off the wall, silencing the sentry before he knew what hit him.

The small amount of noise Sharim's attack produced on the other side of the building made

Mika's guy pause and turn, a frown denting his brow. "Kasim?" he called out. When his buddy didn't answer, he started toward the other side of the building.

Mika waited until he passed directly below her. Then, leaving her rifle on top of the wall, she pushed off, dropped onto the man's back, grabbed his head, yanked it back and sliced into his throat before he could sound the alarm. He slumped beneath her, and she went down with him, her hand still around his neck, her knife buried in his throat and one calf trapped beneath his torso. She fought to free her hand with the knife still in it. Then she rolled onto her back and placed her free foot against the side of the dead man and shoved as hard as she could.

Lance appeared above her, rolled the man off her leg and reached down to pull her to her feet. "Are you all right?"

"Yes." Mika sheathed her knife and reached up to the top of the wall for her rifle. "What did you find?"

"No side entrances." Lance led the way toward Sharim at the rear of the building.

"Same," Ketchum reported into their headsets, coming around the other side at a trot. "It's through the front or the back."

"Back it is." Sharim reached for the door handle of the rear entrance and tried to turn it. "Locked."

Ketchum bent to the man on the ground near his corner and patted his pockets. "Nothing."

Lance hurried back to the man Mika had dispatched and returned, carrying a ring of keys. He inserted one after the other until he found the right one and the door handle turned.

"I'll lead," Ketchum said.

Lance nodded and eased open the door.

Ketchum peered in then entered.

Sharim followed the Delta, and Lance followed Sharim. Mika stayed close behind Lance, covering their rear.

At the first door off the hallway, Ketchum twisted the handle and pushed open the door.

A sound inside indicated occupants. Ketchum fired his rifle with the silencer attached. He took two shots, one right after the other. The clatter of metal on stone sounded loud compared to the *poomph* sound from the silenced rifle.

Lance and Mika took the other side of the hallway. One by one, they cleared the rooms until they reached a T-junction.

Mika led the way to the left, Lance on her heels. Ketchum turned right, with Sharim following the other Delta.

With Lance at her back, Mika moved quickly and silently until the hallway turned right. Voices sounded at the end of this short passage—lots of voices. Too many for the two of them to handle.

"Smoke and Ice, we could use a diversion," Ketchum whispered.

A long moment passed before Smoke responded with, "How soon?"

"ASAP," Ketchum said.

An explosion rocked the ground beneath Mika's feet.

Shouts sounded, and footsteps pounded toward the front of the building,

Some footsteps raced directly for where Mika stood at the corner of the hallway.

Lance rushed up beside her at the exact second a man dressed in black ran around the corner.

Lance raised his rifle in a swift uppercut, slamming the butt into the man's nose, driving his cartilage into his brain. The man fell to his knees.

Mika struck him with her weapon in the back of the head, finishing the job.

He hit the floor and lay still.

Lance peered around the corner then took off.

Mika raced after him, her heart pounding and adrenaline racing through her system.

They might be charging into a hornet's nest, but she refused to let Lance do it alone.

CHAPTER 9

THE SHORT HALLWAY opened into a larger room, with two hallways leading to the rear and a large foyer open to the front of the building. The walls were covered in elaborate and colorful mosaic tile designs. The furnishings consisted of rich, red velvet cushions with gold trim.

Men dressed entirely in black with black turbans wrapped around their heads carried AK-47s. Some rushed for the front entrance. Two of the men hurried toward a doorway close to the short hallway where Lance and Mika were positioned.

When they saw the two there, they skidded to a halt and raised their weapons.

Lance dropped one before he had a chance to pull the trigger or shout. The other man fell beside him, shot in the back.

Sharim and Ketchum emerged from the far hallway.

Mika ducked around him and ran for the door the two Hamas soldiers had been running toward.

Sharim and Ketchum hurried across the room.

From the shouts and gunfire outside, the other Hamas fighters were occupied with the IDF and Deltas raining hell onto them.

With her hand on the doorknob, Mika waited for Sharim's okay to open.

He shook his head, touched a finger to his lips and called out loudly in Arabic.

"What did he say?" Lance asked.

Mika responded. "We are surrounded. We must move you to a safe location."

From inside, a voice shouted back.

Mika interpreted, whispering, "What is the password?"

Standing away from the door, Mika reached out and tested the handle. It was locked.

"Get back," Sharim warned.

She dropped the handle and moved away.

The voice inside shouted again. Seconds later, gunfire sounded, and bullets pierced the door in rapid succession. When they stopped, Ketchum fired at the lock, splintering the doorframe.

Lance stepped in front of the door and kicked his foot hard, hitting just below the doorknob. He jumped back as the door swung open.

More bullets blasted through the doorway and the wall beside it.

Again, the shooting stopped.

"I'll cover," Ketchum said. The older Delta fired through the doorway,

Lance dove beneath the man's weapon, hit the floor and rolled to his feet, weapon raised.

The room was empty; a secret door leading out on the other side swung shut, blending into the wall decoration.

"He's running!" Lance cried out as he leaped over plush cushions, racing for the other side of the room. Mika was right beside him, leaping nimbly over boxes, furnishings and trays of food.

Sharim and Ketchum followed.

At the wall with the hidden door, Lance felt around for the lever to open it, frustrated by the amount of time passing.

Beside him, Mika pushed a red tile in the middle of a wall and the door opened.

"I could kiss you," Lance said. And he did kiss her cheek then ran through the doorway.

A narrow corridor led toward the back of the building.

Lance ran through the passage and arrived at the top of a set of stairs leading downward. He didn't hesitate but ran down them. Motion-sensor lights lighted the tunnel. Some of them blinked out ahead, while the ones they approached blinked to life, lighting their way.

Already, Lance could tell they had gone farther than the length of the compound. The secret passage had to open outside beyond the wall, allowing the occupants a safe way to leave if the compound was breached.

"Deltas," Ketchum called into the radio as he ran, "if any of you can make it to the rear of the compound, our target should be emerging from a hidden tunnel somewhere past the wall."

"On it," Ice responded.

"Me, too," Smoke said. "Gonzo and the others are keeping these guys occupied. They're falling back into the compound. You guys on your way out?"

"Roger," Ketchum said. "Let them hide in the compound. Start falling back to the bikes."

Sharim spoke to his people in Hebrew. In English, he said, "I told my people to hold them while yours get to their motorcycles."

"Can't let you do that," Ketchum said.

"This is our war," Sharim said.

The tunnel ended at a tube shooting straight up with a metal ladder anchored into the wall.

Lance started up, moving as quickly as he could. As he neared the top, which was covered in a round metal hatch, he wondered if Khaled and his men were waiting there to shoot whoever emerged.

"We're at the rear of the compound," Smoke's

voice sounded in his ear. "A black SUV just left a garage a hundred feet from the wall.

"Stop that vehicle," Ketchum shouted.

Lance burst through the hatch, flinging it to the side.

Smoke and Ice were twenty yards ahead of him, firing at and running after the SUV. The vehicle turned onto another road, passed a couple of buildings and disappeared.

"Get to your motorcycles," Ketchum shouted.

Knowing he couldn't outrun a vehicle, Lance headed for the edge of town where he and Mika had stashed their bikes.

Mika kept up with him, zig-zagging through the streets and emerging on the southern edge of town.

Red taillights shone in the distance on the road they'd traversed on their way up.

Lance threw the tree branch to the side, leaped onto his bike and started the engine. Noise didn't matter now. Hamas knew they were there.

"Our bogey is headed south. Mika and I are following," he said into his mic.

"We'll be right behind you."

Mika started the motorcycle beside him and goosed the throttle, sending the bike skidding sideways for a few feet before she righted it and shot forward.

Lance raced after her, catching up and moving up to ride side by side.

In the distance, the red taillights glowed, taunting them and luring them away from the others. But they couldn't let Khaled get away. Lives depended on them taking him out of commission—lives of women and children who had nothing to do with what had happened to Khaled's family.

Slowly, they gained on the SUV ahead of them.

As they approached a village ahead, the SUV turned off the main highway onto a side road heading west.

Without headlights, Lance and Mika followed at a distance.

"Ketchum?" Lance spoke into his radio. "You back there?"

When he received no response, he tried again. "Smoke? Ice? Gonzo? Anyone?"

"Sharim?" Mika's voice sounded in Lance's ear.

No other voices responded on the radio.

"They won't know which way we turned," Mika said.

Lance eased back on the throttle. "We should wait until they get to the village."

"If I wasn't with you, would you turn back?" Mika asked.

He wanted to lie and tell her yes. "No."

"Do what you want. I'm not letting that bastard get away." She gunned her throttle, leaving him behind.

Lance opened the throttle and raced to catch up to the hard-headed woman. He couldn't fault her for doing something he would have done if he'd been in her position. And he was certain she was mad that he would back off because of her. She'd fought hard to be considered an equal with the men she fought alongside.

She was equal in her fighting ability, tactical planning and weapon mastery. But she wasn't a man, and Lance was glad. Mika was a strong, independent woman who was quickly seizing his heart. He couldn't stand the thought of her being injured, killed, captured and tortured. He'd do anything to keep that from happening. He'd do anything to keep any member of his team from the same fate.

The difference was, he didn't want to get naked and make love to the men on his team. He did want to make love with Mika.

When they got through this mission alive, he'd find a way to make that happen, assuming she was willing, of course. He'd woo her as she deserved. She might fight like a man and want to fit in with her special forces brothers, but there was a woman inside her fierce exterior who had let him hold her hand and spoon her body through the night on a hard floor.

For now, they were cut off from the others in enemy territory, following a particularly evil man capable of torturing them and using them as a warning to others to stay away from him or suffer the same fate.

He wished he had comms with his teammates in the Black Hawk. Then at least, he could get them to gun down the SUV. Unfortunately, the SUV had gotten away from town before they could call in backup.

Without a map to guide them, they were at the mercy of the darkness and the taillights of the vehicle in front of them to keep them going.

"Are you okay?" Lance cast a glance toward Mika.

She nodded. "I am."

"Rethinking this madness?"

Mika hesitated for a moment. "No. We'll figure out what to do once he stops. Until then, we stay the course."

"We should be getting close to the border of the West Bank," he said.

"I thought of that. If he passes through, we'll be able to identify yet another breach in the fence as well as have him in our territory. We can find help on the other side."

Assuming Khaled crossed the border and hadn't arranged for someone to fly him across to Gaza. That would be an entirely different effort to extract him.

"Whatever we do, we can't let him get to Gaza," Mika said.

"Woman, are you adding mindreading to your list of skills?"

She chuckled. "It doesn't take a mind reader to figure that one out. Gaza is a hotbed no one wants to touch."

The SUV slowed suddenly, catching them off guard.

Then the lights disappeared as if into thin air.

"What the hell," Lance muttered. "Slow down."

Together, they slowed to a stop at a turn in the road and killed their engines.

Though the road turned, the SUV had not, proceeding half a mile further on a dirt road that led straight into a hillside. In the light from the stars overhead, the hill appeared to be intact. No cave or overhead doors could be seen from their vantage point.

"On foot?" Lance dismounted, knowing her answer.

Mika swung her leg over the motorcycle and pushed it off the road into a shallow ravine.

Lance moved his into the same ravine and piled brush on top.

They set off, moving parallel to the dirt road amongst whatever shadows they could find in the desolate surroundings.

As he neared the hillside, Lance slowed and crouched low to the ground. If this was a hideout for Hamas, there would be guards. He didn't want them to see Mika and him coming. Surprise was their greatest weapon at this point.

Lance pulled out the monocular he kept stowed in his breast pocket and studied the hill, the light from the stars casting confusing shadows around the base of the hill. After staring at the hill for a few minutes, he could make out a massive boulder in front that appeared to have fallen from the bluffs above and rolled to a stop a short distance from the base.

At first, Lance couldn't see that it was guarded. When he started to move closer, Mika grabbed his arm and pointed to the side of the boulder in the deepest shadows.

He didn't see anything. Then the shadow moved, a man dressed in black disengaged from the shadows and rounded to the back of the rock. Seconds later, he reappeared.

Mika pointed to the top of the hill. "And there," she whispered into her mic.

Along the top of the bluff, a dark round silhouette broke the ridgeline. It moved, rising just a little, exposing the shape of shoulders.

Keeping low, Mika and Lance circled the hill, looking for more guards. Out in the middle of nowhere, hiding in a hillside that appeared to be nothing more than a rocky outcropping with no redeeming qualities, who would think to look behind a boulder for a cave entrance?

Apparently, Hamas had.

"We're still too far away from the border for this

hill to hide a tunnel," Mika said. "Khaled is in there. I'd bet my life on it."

"The question is...now what?"

They'd worked their way back around to the front of the hill, closer this time and in the shadows, so the sniper on the hilltop couldn't see to shoot them. They only had to worry about the man in the shadows beside the boulder.

Not knowing how many might be inside the hill, they could either wait for Khaled to emerge and go after him then or take their chances and get inside.

"You want to go in, don't you?" Lance sighed.

"How else will we know for sure whether Khaled is in there?"

"We have no backup, no way to get back across the border."

"We'll find a way." Mika turned toward the eastern sky. "If we're going to do this, we need to do it while it's dark outside. Daylight will leave us far too exposed."

Lance glanced to the sky. Gray light spread across the horizon, dimming the stars to the east. "If we need to move during the dark, we might already be too late."

"Then let's go." Mika rose from where they'd been crouching on the ground and started for the boulder.

Lance grabbed her hand and held her back. "Wait. I see headlights."

Mika flattened herself against the ground.

Lance did the same as the headlights approached. They'd come to rest out of sight of the guards but not of vehicles approaching the hill.

Keeping their heads down as close to the ground as possible, they watched as a truckload of armed men drove straight up to the boulder and then disappeared around the giant curtain it created.

"I guess storming the hill is out of the question now," Mika said.

"For the moment," Lance said, slightly relieved they weren't rushing into a cave full of who knew what. He was all for watching and waiting for a better opportunity to get Khaled. One that didn't involve a dozen to two odds. "At the very least, we should wait until nightfall. The sun will be up within the hour. We might as well rest, watch and wait."

Mika lay stiffly beside him, her lips pressed into a tight line. She wanted to storm in and bring the mission to a satisfactory end with Khaled captured or dead.

Lance wanted that, too. But they couldn't do it alone without studying the situation, getting their bearings and counting the number of bogeys they would have to contend with. Even then, they might be in way over their heads.

For now, they needed food and rest to keep up their strength.

"Let's find a place where we can watch the comings and goings and not be seen in the daylight."

The eastern sky turned a vivid orange as Lance and Mika settled into a rocky crevice that would provide a good vantage point as well as shade during the day.

Far enough away from the guards that they wouldn't be heard, Lance and Mika removed their helmets and body armor, settling in for a day of observation and rest.

"I'll take the first watch while you sleep," he whispered.

"I can't sleep. I'm too wound up," she said, setting with her rifle across her lap.

"Then you take first watch while I sleep." He settled with his back against a rock and closed his eyes.

"How can you sleep sitting up?" she asked.

"I've learned to sleep anywhere in any position." He grinned with his eyes still closed. "Purely out of self-preservation."

He crossed his arms over his chest and drew in a deep breath, letting it out slowly, along with the tension that had been building since they'd landed in the West Bank of Israel. Separated from their teams, just the two of them trapped on a hillside until the sun set again, he could do nothing to fix the situation but get some rest. When the time was right, they'd make a move. Whether it was to get back to their motorcycles to get the hell out of Palestine or to storm the cave where Khaled was hiding, he wasn't sure yet.

One thing was for certain, he couldn't let Mika face the terrorist alone. The woman was bent on proving herself as a member of the IDF special forces; she was downright dangerous to herself and others. Trying to take on a terrorist as unstable and dangerous as Khaled Aziz wasn't the best idea. Trying to bring him in when all they had was the two of them to deal with Khaled and his henchmen...

That was beyond insane.

It might be crazy, but Lance knew without a doubt they'd be sneaking into the cave sometime that day or late into that night. He and Mika had a mission to accomplish, with or without the rest of their team.

He prayed they'd survive.

CHAPTER 10

MIKA SAT QUIETLY AS the sun rose over the hill and beat down on the hilltop. She spent the hours Lance slept studying everything about the man's face, body build and the way he slept with a half-smile teasing the corners of his lips. She enjoyed watching him sleep.

He slept with such abandon, his mouth and eyes twitching as if he was listening to something funny.

Around midday, after sitting for so long with no other activity, Mika had experienced enough boredom to last a lifetime. And she was sleepy. Desperately sleepy. The problem was, she didn't want to admit it. That would be admitting she was weak. And, dammit, she didn't like accepting any kind of weakness.

She nodded off for the third time in an hour, finally admitting to herself that she needed sleep.

"Ready for me to take the watch?" Lance asked, his eyes slits, his lips curling.

"You know I am," she said. Her eyes narrowed. "How long have you been watching me?"

"Long enough to count the three times you've closed your eyes in less than ten minutes." He pushed to an upright sitting position and stretched. "Your turn to get some sleep."

As tired as she was, she was afraid she'd miss something important. "I really need to stay..." a yawn nearly split her face in two, "...awake."

He patted the space beside him. "Quit fighting it and give your body and mind a break. You need the rest to be at your peak performance when we make our move. Lack of sleep can dull your senses and slow your response time."

"I know," she said and yawned again. The warm sun only made her sleepier. "Okay," she grumbled. "I'll sleep, but only for a few minutes."

"Good girl." He moved over, allowing her to stretch out fully on the ground beside him.

She did, closing her eyes immediately. "Wake me up if anything happens," she said, her voice fading off as she drifted into the deep, dreamless sleep of the completely exhausted.

When she woke, it took her several minutes to get her bearings. She lay with her cheek resting against Lance's chest and her arm draped over his torso. She tilted her head back to look up into his face, expecting to see him sound asleep as well. How else could she have ended up all over this man she barely knew?

Though shocked by her instinctive gravitation toward the man and his deliciously solid body, she didn't move right away. The sleep had left her wanting more.

And her mind and thoughts weren't thinking about more sleep. She wanted more with Lance. More snuggles. More of her body pressed against his. More of her skin touching his skin. More kisses and a chance to make love with the Delta in a bed, not on a rocky hill.

Not that she was making love to him. Not when they were in danger because they'd followed a known terrorist to his lair and then hung out, waiting for him to do something stupid. Now was not the time to lust after a man. Hell, she was in uniform. That fact, by itself, should have made her think twice.

Well, it did. It made her think of how wonderful it would be to get out of that uniform and strip the clothes off Lance and crawl all over his body.

Her fingers curled into the fabric of his uniform jacket.

"Hey." His chest rumbled beneath her ear. "Awake?"

She nodded, still pressed against him. "How long?"

"Four hours."

That made her sit up and frown. "Four hours?" She pushed her hair back from her face and stared through the gap in the rocks to the guard standing in the shadow of the giant boulder. "Did I miss anything?"

He shook his head. "Not a damn thing."

"Should we try our radios again?" She reached for her helmet.

"I did a few minutes ago, hoping the others might wander into range." His lips formed a thin line.

"Nothing." Mika sighed. Not that she expected to have contact with the others. Not when they'd gone so far and were now stuck in the middle of nowhere. "Too bad we don't have a cellphone."

"I have one." He shook his head. "No reception."

Her stomach rumbled. Mika pressed a hand to her belly.

Lance dug his hand into one of the pockets on the side of his trousers, pulled out a granola bar and handed it to her.

Mika frowned and held up her hands, refusing to take his offering. "I can't take your food. Besides, I have some of my own." She searched her pockets and found the protein bar she'd stashed there for a quick energy pickup. She tore open the bar, broke off a third and wrapped the rest, storing it in her pocket for later.

Lance did the same, eating a third of his granola bar then returning the remainder to his pocket.

"I don't want to think this might take another day, but…" Mika shrugged.

With a nod, Lance finished her thought. "It pays to be prepared."

As long as they had water, they'd be okay for a few days. Mika sipped from the straw leading to the camelback water storage device she wore like a backpack. She chewed the protein bar slowly, not knowing when they'd get a chance to eat their next meal. Hell, she wasn't even certain when they'd get back across the border into friendly territory.

As far as she was concerned, their number one priority was to end Khaled's terror against her teammates' families.

The sun slipped lower on the horizon, and dusk crept around the rocky hillside. As darkness descended, an engine rumbled to life, the sound echoing off the rocky surface of the bluff. Minutes later, a truck emerged from behind the boulder. In the murky light, Mika counted eight soldiers in the back.

"Eight of the twelve," Lance murmured beside her, his monocular pressed to his eye. "Makes the odds a little better."

She nodded. "As long as they didn't leave with Khaled."

"I didn't see him in the front of the truck, and he wasn't in the rear." Lance handed her the monocular.

Mika studied the truck as it left the hill and

headed east on the main road. She couldn't make out faces, but her gut told her Khaled was still close by.

He had to be. They had a job to do. Khaled was the critical component necessary to complete it.

They waited quietly, watching for movement from the hideout. After several hours had passed and the hour grew late, Lance touched Mika's arm.

She looked up at him in the starlight. "Game time?"

He nodded.

They slipped into their body armor, checked their weapons and communications devices, and counted the number of magazines filled with ammo. They had everything they could possibly need to fight a battle except the backup and support of the rest of their team.

They were on their own.

"We don't have to do this, you know." Lance cupped her cheek and stared down into her eyes. "We can head back to the extraction point and hope the team will come looking for us there."

She laid her hand over his and turned, pressing her lips to his palm. When she looked up, she felt as if she could drown in his gaze. This man was beginning to mean so much more than just a teammate. "We know where Khaled is. If we leave, he might relocate. We can't miss this chance. If we do, how many more families will be destroyed?"

He sighed. "Okay, but let's recon before we commit. We don't know what we're up against."

She nodded. "Agreed. We just have to get past that guard on the ground and the one on the bluff."

"We can do that."

"But we can't take either one of them out without committing to the rest of the mission," she said, holding his gaze.

"True. Which makes it more difficult to perform our reconnaissance."

Mika stared down at the body armor and the helmet in her hand. "We should go in light, with nothing that rattles or makes noises that could alert the guard."

Lance nodded. "Handguns and knives. We leave the rest here."

Mika shrugged out of her body armor and laid aside her helmet. "We won't have our radios without our helmets," she pointed out.

"Then we have to stay together and use hand signals."

With their rifles, spare magazines and helmets grounded, Mika felt naked but more agile and able to move silently in the night.

They slipped out of their hiding place and crept up to the base of the hill, careful to cling to shadows to remain out of view of the sentry positioned on the bluff.

When they were within twenty yards of the guard

standing at the base of the boulder, they paused, looking for an opportunity to slip past him.

For what felt like an eternity, the guard remained at his post, unmoving.

When Mika was ready to blow her cover, take out the guard and get moving, the man turned and walked behind the boulder.

Lance slipped past her, sprinted across the open and plastered himself against the boulder.

Before the guard could return, Mika darted out and joined Lance against the boulder, her back to the rock, her heart pounding against her ribs.

Lance inched around to the back of the giant rock. Mika followed close on his heels.

A large overhead door had been installed in the face of the hill, with a smaller door beside it.

Deeply shadowed by the giant boulder, the doors were barely discernible. If her sight hadn't already adjusted to the lack of available light, Mika might not have believed what she was seeing.

The smaller door stood open a crack. The guard must have gone inside.

Lance crossed to the face of the rock and stood in the darkness, his back against the hillside.

Mika joined him and froze at the sound of footsteps echoing inside the cave.

The door swung open, and the guard emerged, talking into a hand-held radio he had pressed against his ear. He strode past Lance without looking in his direction.

Lance and Mika waited to move until the guard disappeared around the other side of the boulder to resume his position.

Lance tiptoed to the door and twisted the handle. It didn't turn, but the door hadn't closed properly. He was able to push it open a crack and peer inside, and then he stepped through it.

With her heart in her throat, Mika eased up to the door, waiting for any sign that Lance had been discovered.

A scraping sound behind her made her step through the door and inside a tunnel large enough for vehicles to enter. The darkness was so complete, she couldn't see her hand in front of her face.

Ahead, a dim light glowed, barely penetrating the gloom.

A shadow moved, blocking the light.

A scream rose in her throat. Before it escaped her lips, a hand clamped over her mouth.

"Shh," Lance whispered. "It's me."

Of course, it was. Mika willed her heartbeat to slow to a normal pace.

Lance led her to the end of the tunnel, where it opened into a large cavern. The soft glowing light was from a lantern perched on top of a wooden crate at the far end of the cavern. It illuminated a structure built into the cave. Several doors lined the back wall, but it was what was between the entrance and the rooms at the rear that held Mika's attention.

Long wooden crates stood in rows, some stacked four and five crates high. The black SUV was parked near the rear beside a large cargo truck and several pickups.

Lance crossed to one of the crates nearest to them. The top had been pried loose and propped against the side. He shined a small flashlight into the box and stiffened.

Mika leaned up on her toes to look over the edge into the crate and swallowed hard on a gasp. Inside were long, slender, sand-colored missiles. She'd seen pictures of these missiles in training. They looked like the Fajr3 missiles Iran had been selling to the Palestinian Islamic Jihad in Gaza. So far, Gaza had been the only place they'd been discovered. But here they were in the West Bank.

Her chest squeezed hard as she looked around the inside of the cave at the longer crates, possibly containing Fajr5 missiles.

There were so many.

Mika's stomach roiled.

One of the doors at the back of the cave opened, and light spilled out.

Lance clicked off the light and ducked below the top of the crate.

Mika sank to a crouch and inched toward the end of the box to peer around its edge. She had a straight shot to the open door, where several men emerged. Three carried rifles, four more did not. They were talking, but Mika was too far from them to hear their words. When they were finished, two of the unarmed men climbed into a truck. The three armed men climbed into the truck bed. The engine started, and headlights blinked on.

Mika closed one eye to keep from losing all her night vision.

Lance said close to her ear over the engine's rumble, "We need to get out of here."

"What about all of this?" Mika tipped her head toward the crates.

"That's why we need to get out of here. Now." He moved back behind the wooden box, pulling her with him as the truck's headlights chased away the shadows around them.

One of the armed men jumped from the truck's bed and opened the overhead door, rolling it upward until it was high enough for the truck to exit.

After the truck pulled through, the gunman lowered the door from the other side, sealing Lance and Mika inside the cave in darkness.

A door closed at the far end of the cave.

Lance moved to the end of the crate and waited, watching the doors at the end. Mika looked over his shoulder, both eyes open. One still adjusting to the darkness all over again.

After several long seconds, Lance darted toward the smaller door and eased it open.

"The truck stopped on the other side of the boulder," Lance said. "I can see its brake lights. If we want out of here, we need to move now."

He didn't wait for her response. Ducking through the door, he ran for the backside of the boulder. Mika followed and looked up to the top of the bluff. She couldn't see the guard up there. He probably had a better view of the area in front of the boulder.

The truck stayed for several more minutes before it pulled away; the engine noise faded until silence again reigned.

Mika braced herself, ready to leap into action should the guard round the corner of the boulder and discover them standing there. She listened for sounds from within the cave. They'd be trapped if either of the cave entrance doors opened and more people emerged from inside.

The doors didn't open behind them. Eventually, the guard came around the corner of the boulder and strode straight to the small door. He didn't look around, completely missing Lance and Mika for a second time.

Mika didn't question their luck, just waited until the door closed behind the guard and hurried after Lance when he ran for the shadows at the base of the hill.

They worked their way back to their hiding place

in the crevice between the rocks, neither speaking until they were safely hidden.

Mika collapsed to the ground, overwhelmed by what they'd witnessed. "We have a bigger problem than any of us originally imagined."

Lance nodded. "The question is…what are we going to do about it?"

Mika stared across the narrow space between them and shook her head. "We can't let it go. We can't walk away."

"We don't have the means to destroy it," he countered.

"Maybe not," she said, "but, maybe, we can keep it from leaving the cave."

CHAPTER 11

"I LIKE THE WAY YOU THINK," Lance leaned forward and pressed a kiss to Mika's lips.

She smiled, reached across, wrapped her hands around the back of his neck and pulled him close again, deepening the kiss.

He thrust his tongue past her teeth to claim hers in a long, sensual caress that made his groin tighten and his blood burn through his veins.

Adrenaline still hummed through his system; he couldn't stop there. He ran his hands down her sides and pulled her body against his. Abandoning her mouth, he trailed kisses along her jaw and down the length of her neck to where her pulse beat at the base.

Mika moaned and leaned into him, her hands sliding over his shoulders and down to his waist, where she pulled his T-shirt out of the waistband of his trousers. Once the hem was free, she ran her fingers beneath the fabric and up over his skin, blazing a trail of fire.

He reached for her uniform jacket and flicked the buttons open, frustrated with how long it was taking. Finally, he grabbed the hem and dragged the jacket over her head and tossed it to the side. The T-shirt beneath was next, leaving her upper body exposed to the starlight, turning her skin a sexy shade of indigo blue.

Mika flicked open the buttons on his uniform jacket and pushed it from his shoulders. Then she ran her hands over his T-shirt-covered chest, angling downward to grab the hem and drag it up the length of his torso and over his head.

Lance claimed her lips again, kissing her hard while his hands slid down her back and around to cup her breasts. "This is insane," he said against her lips. "You deserve better than sex on a bed of rocks."

"So do you," she murmured. "But it looks like it's just the two of us on this mission. If we don't make it out, I don't want any regrets." She pressed her lips to his then traced a path from his chin to his chest and down to one of his hard brown nipples.

Lance slid her bra straps from her shoulders.

Mika reached behind her, unhooked the clasps. Her full, gorgeous breasts fell free of the garment, tempting Lance beyond redemption.

Grabbing his jacket and hers, he spread them out

on the flattest surface and eased Mika down on her back.

She laced her fingers behind his neck and pulled him close for a kiss.

Lance couldn't get enough of her. He kissed her long and hard. When he came up for air, he vowed to taste as much of her as possible in the short amount of time they had on that hill. If they didn't live to tomorrow, they'd die sated from making love.

He kissed a path down her neck, across a sexy shoulder and back to take one luscious breast in his mouth. Sucking it between his teeth, he pulled gently then rolled the nipple with his tongue until it hardened into a tight little bead. Moving to the other breast, he gave it equal attention as Mika writhed beneath him.

While he tasted and teased her breasts, Mika worked the zipper on her trousers, easing it down. She slipped her hand beneath her panties and stroked herself.

Lance swallowed a groan, ready to take the place of her hand with his. He'd been taking it slow, allowing her the chance to get used to the idea of making love with him. Maybe she didn't need as much time as he'd thought. He covered her hand with his, cupping her sex. When she pulled her fingers free, he took over.

Sliding a finger between her folds, he sank a finger into her center.

Sweet heaven. He found her channel warm and slick. She was more than ready.

His cock swelled, straining against the fabric of his trousers.

Mika flicked the button open at his waist, lowered his zipper and captured his erection as it sprang free of its constraints.

Her hand wrapped around him, sliding to the base and up again.

With his fingers inside her, all wet and warm, and her hand caressing his dick, he wasn't sure how long he could hold back. Determined to pleasure her first, he pulled free of her hand and lowered himself over her, kissing and nipping his way to her waistband. She reached down to push her trousers lower.

He helped, pulling off her boots, and then her pants. When Mika lay on the jackets completely naked, her skin glowing in the starlight, Lance could barely breathe.

"Beautiful," he whispered.

She gave a strangled laugh and shook her head. "Make love to me," she said, her voice soft, gravelly and so sexy, Lance had to comply.

He took a breast in his mouth and sucked hard. Then he moved downward, settling between her thighs.

Mika weaved her fingers in his hair, raising her hips off the ground.

Lance trailed a finger along the sensitive skin of

her inner thigh up to her center. There, he slid a finger inside her and swirled it around

A soft moan sounded as Mika rocked her hips.

Pressing another finger in with the first, he pumped slowly, gently.

The fingers in his hair tightened their hold, tugging in spasms. He eased his fingers out and concentrated on her pleasure center. Using his thumbs, he parted her folds and blew a stream of air over the small knot of tightly bundled nerves.

Mika sucked in a sharp breath.

Lance tapped that nubbin with the tip of his tongue.

Her knees rose around his ears, and her heels braced against the ground.

As he licked her there, her hips rose off the ground and her back arched.

"Yes," she said. "Please."

He chuckled and flicked her clit again, swirling his tongue around and around it until she bucked beneath him.

Her body went rigid with her release.

He didn't slow his movement until she collapsed back against the ground, her breathing ragged, a smile curving her lips.

Her fingers tightened in his hair, dragging him up her body. "I want you, Lance Rankin. Inside me. Now," she whispered, reaching down to tug his trousers down his thighs.

Without waiting for him to strip off his boots or pants, she guided him toward her center.

When his cock nudged her entrance, he paused. "Hang on."

Her fingers dug into his buttocks. "What? Why?"

"Protection." He dug into his back pocket and pulled out a foil packet.

She chuckled. "Do you always carry condoms into battle?"

He shook his head. "No. Actually, I was thinking of you when I slid that into my back pocket. Like a lucky charm. If we made it out of this unscathed, I was going to woo you until you consented to let me use this."

She took the packet from him. "Do men always talk this much during sex?"

"I don't usually."

"Are you nervous?" she asked.

"A little. I don't want you to think I'm only after sex."

She raised a dark eyebrow. "Are you?"

"No way." He leaned down and brushed a kiss across her lips. "I want more than a one-night stand."

"What if all I want is sex?" she asked, holding the condom hostage until he answered.

"Then I'll have to work harder to convince you otherwise."

She smiled, tore open the package, pulled out the condom and rolled it over his engorged staff. When she was finished, she gripped his hips in her hands and positioned him at her entrance. "I look forward to the amount of effort you will employ. Now, shut up and make love to me before we're found with our pants down."

With his cock dipping into her juices, Lance could hold back no longer. With as much control as he could muster, he eased into her, giving her time to adjust to his girth.

Her hands clamped down on his buttocks and slammed him all the way home, sheathing his entire length in her moist warmth.

For a moment, he held still. Then he moved, slowly at first, increasing his speed as the fire built inside.

Soon, he pounded in and out of her.

Mika raised her hips, matching each of his thrusts.

Tension built low in his groin and feathered outward, his entire body reverberating with his raging desire until he jettisoned over the edge. On his last thrust, he sank deep inside her and remained there, his member throbbing with wave upon wave of his release.

Finally spent, he dropped down to steal a kiss, and then pulled out of her, peeled off the condom and laid down beside her, gathering her in his arms. "I promise that next time, we'll have a proper bed."

He kissed her forehead and took her lips gently. "I never wanted our first time to be like this."

"What was wrong with this?" she asked. "Adrenaline-induced-lust can be the best." She smiled at him and brought his hand up to cup her breast. "My only regret is that we can't do it again right now."

Lance gathered her closer. "You're a remarkable woman. I don't want what we shared tonight to be the last time. I will figure out a way for us to be together."

She sighed. "Let's get through tonight before you make any promises."

He touched a finger to her lips. "Just one, then."

Her brow wrinkled. "Okay."

"I promise to get you out of this alive."

A frown dented her forehead. "We don't know how this is going to end up. You shouldn't make a promise like that. It could bring bad luck."

"I like to think we make our own luck." He lifted her hand to his lips and pressed a kiss into her palm. "That's for you to carry with you. I'll give you more when this mission is done."

Her brow remained furrowed. "If you're going to promise me anything, promise me that you will not die trying to keep me alive."

He stared into her eyes. "I can't make that promise. If it's a choice between my life or yours…I'm going to make the only choice I can." He gave her a gentle smile.

"But don't worry. I'm not ready to leave this earth yet. I have a whole lot more of this I want to do before I go." He smacked her bare bottom softly. "Get dressed. We need a plan and to make it happen tonight, if at all possible. I'm hungry and don't want to stay on this hillside another night. There's a bed somewhere in Jerusalem where we're going to make love like regular people."

He helped her dress in the clothes she'd shed earlier and got himself back into his.

"Let's go through what we have." He laid out the vest containing his body armor and ammunition in front of him and started going through it. It felt like a decade had passed since he'd loaded the vest with everything he might need to pick off Khaled. In the vest, he found four magazines full of bullets for his rifle, three smaller ones for his pistol, a fragmentation grenade and a smoke grenade.

"The grenade could cause some damage, but I'm not sure it would be enough to seal the tunnel," Mika said.

"At best, it has a three-second delay. Not enough to set it off among the missiles and let us get out before all hell breaks loose."

Mika shook her head. "I don't want to think what kind of damage igniting all those missiles might cause. If we could at least find a way to seal the tunnel into the cave, we could keep those missiles from getting into the wrong hands. What we need is explosives sufficient to shut down that tunnel leading into the cave."

Lance patted his jacket pockets.

Mika laughed. "Got another condom in there?"

"No, but I have what we're looking for." His hands moved from his jacket pockets to those on the legs of his trousers. Each side had something in it. His pulse kicked up as he fished the contents out of the left pocket to discover the first-aid kit he always carried. Switching to the other pocket, his hand curled around a cool, squishy lump.

He grinned as he pulled out a pound of C4 explosive putty. Then he dug deeper in the same pocket and pulled out a remote detonator. "I thought I'd packed some clay. I never know when I might need to blow up something."

Mika's lips twisted. "That's not enough to bring down the tunnel."

"You're right. But it might be enough to help block the tunnel sufficiently to keep anyone from getting in or out with those missiles."

Mika's brow smoothed. "What do you have in mind?" Mika asked. "Shall we start a landslide from the top and hope it blocks the entrance? Or take our chances and wedge the C4 into a crevice in the ceiling of the tunnel?"

He leaned forward and kissed her full on the lips. "If I didn't love you so much, I'd be scared of you."

Lance leaned forward, thinking out loud. "I don't want to count on budging enough rock in a landslide to seal the tunnel. The big boulder in front was the last natural landslide, and it didn't do the job. I do like the idea of wedging the C-4 into the ceiling of the tunnel."

"That's not nearly enough explosive compound to bring it down."

"No, it's not. But if we block the tunnel first then set off an explosion, maybe it will be enough to keep Khaled from moving his missiles before the IDF can decide what to do with them."

"What do you have in mind for blocking the tunnel?"

"You know that big truck and the SUV would be just about enough to jam the entrance if wrecked appropriately. We might not even need the explosives."

Mika's lips turned upward. "That might work. It would be even better if Khaled were trapped inside."

"Exactly." Lance tucked the C4 back into his pocket and checked his watch. "We have approximately six more hours until dawn. If we're going to do this, we need to get in place."

"Do you know how to hotwire a vehicle?" Mika asked.

"I might be able to. What would be great is if they left the keys in the ignition."

"Ha."

Lance shrugged. "You never know. We'll start with that assumption and adjust fire as needed."

"We'll set the explosives in the tunnel before we stir them up by stealing their vehicles. That's sure to wake them."

Mika nodded. "We'll have to coordinate starting the engines and be ready to do it simultaneously."

"We can use the grenades to buy us some time to get the vehicles to the other end of the cave."

It would be risky, and Lance didn't like that they didn't have anyone for a backup. "If we get in there and can't get the vehicles started, we'll leave and come up with a different plan. Deal?"

When Mika hesitated, Lance pressed. "I won't leave you in that cave. If you stay, I stay."

"Fine," Mika said. "If we can't start the trucks, we'll get out, regroup and come up with another plan."

"In the meantime, the explosives will be set in the ceiling of the tunnel. If we plant them close to the doors, it will take Khaled time to clear the debris. We could be back on the other side of the fence by then and alert the IDF that there's a stockpile of missiles just across the border."

They gathered the items they'd need, slipped into their body armor and helmets and left their rifles behind.

"Are we going to take out the guards?" Mika asked.

"If things don't go according to plan and we can't use the vehicles to block the tunnel, we need to get back out of the cave undetected. Eliminating the guard by the boulder might make it easier to get into the cave, but it would destroy our chances of getting out without anyone the wiser. As soon as they discover the guard's body, they'll put everyone on high alert."

"Don't kill the guard," Mika said with a nod. "Got it."

They moved down the side of the hill, waited in the shadows for the boulder guard to take a break and moved in, hunkering low beside the door, waiting for the guard to exit.

When he did, Lance held his breath. Surely, the guy wouldn't be dumb enough to walk past without seeing them again.

But he did.

Letting go of the breath he'd been holding, Lance eased through the door into the tunnel.

When he was sure he was alone, he pulled open the door and Mika slipped through.

He hurried to the end of the tunnel, where it opened into the cave.

Voices sounded ahead, along with the sound of hammering.

Staying in the shadows, Lance and Mika stared

out at the rows and rows of crates filled with missiles.

Several men stood around with rifles while one wielded a sledgehammer and a crowbar, working at removing the lid from the crate.

"Time to regroup," Lance whispered.

Mika stood beside him, her eyes on the man standing behind the ones with the guns. "That's Khaled. He's standing behind the others."

Lance squinted at the man half-hidden by the men bearing arms.

The silvery-white hair gave him away. He was the man who'd gone on the news to deliver his threat to all those who'd helped free Yaron.

Mika's hand went to the pistol she had in a holster strapped to her thigh.

Lance touched her arm and motioned for her to back down the tunnel.

For a long moment, Mika didn't move.

"If you kill him now, we won't live to warn the people of Israel of what they have here."

Finally, she nodded and backed away from the cave.

They turned and hurried back the way they'd come.

As they reached the small door, the large overhead door shot upward, and a moving truck backed in through the open entrance,

Lance and Mika shrank against the tunnel wall

next to the smaller door. When it opened as well, they were hidden behind it.

The boulder guard hurried through the tunnel while the big truck slowly eased all the way into the tunnel, guided by a man carrying an AK47.

Another gunman pulled the overhead door down as the truck continued backing into the cave.

With all their attention on the door, the truck and the cave destination, the men carrying rifles didn't notice the man and woman standing behind the door.

Lance grabbed Mika's hand and whispered into his mic. "Move. Now."

He slipped around the door and out into the open, praying there weren't more gun-toting terrorists outside.

Once they cleared the door, Lance and Mika clung to the shadows and worked their way around the base of the hill, out of view of the bluff guard—and the boulder guard, should he return anytime soon.

Mika dug her heels in the ground, tugged on Lance's hand still holding hers and brought them to a halt. "We can't walk away and do nothing. That truck is there to load something. It has to be the missiles."

Lance nodded. "You're right. We have to stop them. But we can't launch a full-on frontal assault. We're going to Plan B."

"Which is?"

"We're going to attempt to blow that bluff loose to fill in the space between the boulder and the cave entrance."

"What if it doesn't work?" Mika demanded.

"Then one of us needs to be down here to shoot out tires, throw a grenade or otherwise disable the truck to keep it from leaving with those missiles. Do you want to take out the sentry on the bluff and set the charges, or do you want to hang out here and lob a grenade should the truck attempt to leave before I can detonate the explosives?"

Mika lifted her chin. "I'll stay here and see that that truck and Khaled don't leave before you get back down here."

Lance captured her chin in his hand and brushed his thumb over her lip. "Don't try to be a hero. If you don't think you can get that grenade close enough, don't throw it. We'll find another way to stop that truck from getting too far."

Her brow creased. "How? We're on foot until we can get back to our motorcycles. That truck could be a long way down the road before we can attempt to follow it. And that leaves no one to follow Khaled to his next hideout. We cannot let Khaled escape."

"And we can't let anyone deploy those missiles. Either way, lives will be lost."

"Then get going," Mika said. "We may not have much time."

"I'm not going to set off the explosion until I get back down to you."

"I'll be out of the way. Don't worry about me. Just blow up that bluff and stop those men from moving those missiles."

"On it," Lance leaned close. "We're not done, so don't go anywhere without me." Then he kissed her as best he could while both were wearing their helmets. He hated letting her out of his sight, but he had to go, and she had to stay and make sure the missiles didn't leave the cave.

Lance and Mika raced up the hillside to where they'd stashed their rifles. He handed Mika the grenade he had tucked into a pouch on his vest. "See you in a few."

Lance climbed up the side of the hill, fully aware he had to get past the bluff guard before he could set the charges. He hoped he had the element of surprise on his side. The top of the bluff didn't offer much in the way of cover. He'd be exposed long enough for the man to turn his weapon on him.

He couldn't afford to get shot. That would leave Mika with no one to get her out should she be captured or injured. And if she thought she was the last hope to end Khaled's terror and the missiles making it to the wrong hands, she'd do something desperate, even sacrifice herself to save the world.

Lance almost turned around and went back down to Mika, but he was already nearing the top of the hill and would be in sight of the bluff guard in the next few seconds.

The dark silhouette of a man rose from his position at the edge of the bluff. He was facing the road leading up to the face of the hill, his back to Lance.

There was no going back now.

CHAPTER 12

Mika found a perch not far from where the guard leaned against the boulder, holding his weapon cradled in his arms. If she had to, she could toss the grenade from her location and get it close enough to disable a vehicle. If she had to.

In the meantime, she fixed her gaze on the lone guard. With a single bullet from her rifle, she could pick him off. Just one shot with the silencer. She was tempted. All the waiting and watching had her tied up in knots. She needed action.

Her training for Sayeret Matkal had drilled the values of observation and patience into her head. She drew on that training now, counting the minutes until Lance had the explosives in place and got back down the hill to where she was. She didn't want him on that bluff when he detonated the charges. Anything could happen. For all she knew, half the hillside could slide off. Or nothing. In that case, she and Lance could be fighting more than half a dozen terrorists. If that happened...so be it. Her hand tightened on her rifle. She had enough ammunition to hold out for a while. She might even manage to take every last one of the terrorists down.

Fifteen minutes had passed since Lance had left her to climb to the top of the hill. From where she lay, she couldn't see the bluff or the man who guarded it. She couldn't tell if Lance had overcome the guard or if he lay injured, maybe dying. If he didn't come down soon, she'd abandon her post and climb up there to see what had happened. A dozen different scenarios ran through her mind. Her only calming thought was that if he'd had a problem with the guard and the guard won the argument, the guard would have reported the incident to those inside the hill. In that case, they would have sent out reinforcements. The large overhead doors and the regular door remained closed. The boulder guard hadn't taken a break or gone back inside after he'd returned from escorting the truck into the cave. All was still calm.

How long did it take to load missiles into the back of a moving van? How many could they fit? She hoped they were having troubles getting the big wooden crate moved into the van, thus delaying their departure, giving Lance sufficient time to place the explosives, detonator and get back to her.

Her pulse racing, Mika fought to remain still. The more she moved, the more chance she had of being spotted by Khaled's men.

Five minutes later, just when she'd resigned herself to sitting there all night, the overhead door opened.

The dark SUV waited on the other side.

Mika tensed. The vehicle was the same one they'd followed, carrying Khaled Aziz. She pulled the monocular Lance had given her out of her pocket and pressed it to her eye, bringing the people on the ground below into focus. She could see through the front passenger seat of the SUV.

The man inside had silvery-white hair and a neatly trimmed mustache and beard. She raised her rifle to rest against her shoulder and aimed at Khaled Aziz.

Mika brought the monocular back to her eye and twisted the mechanism, bringing the images she was following into crystal clear focus. Yes, indeed, the man in the passenger seat was Khaled. The man was cocky and sure of himself. He lowered the window on his side to speak to the guard. Soon, the window slid upward, and the SUV rolled forward.

It was now or never.

Still, Mika couldn't bring herself to pull the trigger and put a bullet through the man's forehead. As she focused on the terrorist with a price on his head, the cargo truck rolled to a stop behind the SUV.

"Come on, Lance," she whispered into her helmet.

"Almost done," he responded with a chuckle.

Relief flowed through her veins at the sound of his voice. Mika's heart rate increased. That familiar surge of adrenaline spiked through her veins. She would be ready if the SUV moved another inch forward. Balancing her rifle in her hands, she practiced her breathing, holding her weapon steady and touching, but not pulling, the trigger.

"Have you set the charge?" Mika asked into her radio.

"Almost done up here," Lance answered.

At that moment, the SUV rolled forward.

"Khaled is on the move. His SUV just left the tunnel."

"Do what you have to do to make him stop."

Steeling her resolve, Mika shifted her aim from the passenger seat to the tires on the front of the SUV.

As one of the best sharpshooters on her team, she channeled inner calm, aimed, pulled the trigger and pierced the SUV's front right tire. Because her rifle had been equipped with a silencer, there wasn't a sound to accompany the tire being blown out other than the air whooshing free. The SUV stopped, and the driver got out.

The guard joined him to look at the flat tire.

Khaled remained inside the SUV.

As the two men bent to look at the hole in the tire, they appeared to be discussing its cause. After studying the tire a bit longer, they both glanced up to the hillside where Mika lay low, her body pressed to the dirt.

The driver waved to the guard, who started toward the hill while the driver returned to the SUV. A moment later, the reverse lights blinked on the SUV, and it moved back toward the truck.

In turn, the truck backed into the tunnel.

"I shot a hole into the SUV's front tire. They know someone is out here, and they've sent the guard up the hill to find out who."

Half a dozen men emerged from the tunnel, carrying rifles. They aimed for the hill where Mika lay.

"As soon as you can, sweetheart, fire away," she said. "I have company headed my way. One guard wasn't enough. They're sending in reinforcements. I have seven men breathing down my neck."

"Charge set," Lance said, his voice tense. "I'm on my way down."

If she moved, they'd see her. If she stayed put, they'd eventually find her. If she started shooting, they would locate her even sooner. Before the six men could start up the hill, Mika pulled the pin on the grenade and tossed it to the bottom of the hill. It rolled a few feet, landing in the middle of the men with their guns.

Mika covered her head and closed her eyes.

The grenade exploded.

Four of the six men sustained injuries that brought them to a halt. The other two picked themselves up and continued up the hillside.

The boulder guard was almost on Mika when she raised her rifle and fired.

The bullet hit him in the arm, but he didn't slow, and he didn't stop.

Mika pulled the trigger again. This time, the rifle misfired.

She pulled out the magazine and slammed it back in. The gun still would not fire.

With the boulder guard a few short yards away, Mika laid down her rifle, yanked her pistol from the holster on her vest and aimed it at the man's chest.

He dove to the ground.

Mika pulled the trigger a second too late. The bullet completely missed the man.

She fired again, but he'd disappeared behind a rocky outcropping.

Darkness and shadows made it hard for her to follow the man's movements. She could see the other two gunmen as they climbed the hill. She aimed her handgun at one, fired three times and only managed to hit him in the knee once. It was enough to stop him—five down of seven.

"Make that ten," Mika said under her breath as three more armed men stormed out of the building, heading for her.

She fired shots at the gunman already climbing up the hill. He ducked his head, rolled to the side and continued upward.

Mika glanced around, searching for the boulder guard. She had to find him before he found her.

Rounds pinged off the rocky surface beside her from the men below.

She raised her handgun to fire back and changed her mind. Her aim was good, but the handgun's limited range required the target to be much closer.

The Hamas terrorists advanced. When they stopped just short of the range of her pistol, Mika fired anyway.

One man went down; two others scrambled for cover.

The SUV and truck appeared again in the large overhead door.

"Khaled's SUV and the cargo truck are going to make a break for it. They're emerging now from the big door," Mika said into her radio. "Now would be a good time to make some noise."

"Are you far enough away?" Lance asked.

"Yes," she whispered. "Just do it." She wasn't sure if she was far enough way. It didn't matter. What mattered was keeping any of the missiles from leaving the cave. She covered her head, neck and ears and held her breath.

A sudden blast rocked the ground beneath Mika and spewed rocks, dust and debris through the air like projectiles.

The second, larger blast exploded, shaking everything.

Dust nearly obstructed the view of the bluffs above.

A low rumble accompanied the ground shaking beneath her boots.

The rumble grew to a roar. Smaller rocks and gravel slipped free of the bluff. Moments later, the entire bluff sluffed off the side of the hill and crashed down, depositing tons of rock between the giant boulder and the cave entrance. Dust roiled up in a choking cloud that obliterated any kind of view of the hill, the truck and the men attempting to find her.

"Lance?" Mika called out softly, her throat choking on the thick dust particles. "Lance?" Her chest tightened, and she rose from her position, staring around as if she had even a chance of seeing what was going on.

Her most immediate concern was the status of one Delta Force operator who'd risked his life to set off the charges that, hopefully, blocked the truck from leaving with its load of missiles.

Until the dust cleared, she wouldn't be able to

assess the damage to the cave entrance. Until the dust cleared, she wouldn't be able to search for Lance.

A hand grabbed her from behind.

She turned, relief flooding her until she stared into the face of the boulder guard.

He jerked her around and pressed the barrel of a handgun to her temple. "Fight me and die," he stated simply in Arabic.

With a loaded gun pointing at her head, Mika didn't want to push the man's buttons and make him decide she wasn't worth keeping to interrogate. She would bide her time and wait for her chance to break free of her captor. The sooner she did, the better chance she had of finding her man still alive.

The guard took the handgun from her and tossed it aside. With visibility less than two feet, the gloom was hard to penetrate. Mika could have been on a deserted planet or in a crowded city and felt the same sense of being alone, isolated from everyone else except the man holding her hostage.

If Lance were alive, he'd have a hell of a time finding her, or her him. Getting off the hill would be treacherous when he wouldn't be able to see his feet, much less any drop-offs that might be in front of him.

Dust filled Mika's lungs, making it difficult to breathe. The particles floating in the air irritated her eyes. She blinked to clear them, only to add more dust. If the debris caused such a reaction with her, it had to be impacting the man holding the gun to her head. He jerked her arm up behind her, pressing it between her shoulder blades. Mika had to stand on her toes to relieve the pain. She was beginning to regret not taking the shot to kill the man minutes earlier.

He shoved her ahead of him, pushing her down the slope toward the bottom of the hill. If he managed to get her to the base, there might be survivors—men with more guns, less willing to keep her alive. Mika had to make a move to disengage from her captor soon.

Her boot skittered across loose rock, and she suddenly dipped.

The man behind her slipped as well. His grip on her arm loosened just long enough for Mika to duck, spin and butt her head into his gut, sending him flying back to land on his ass. He waved his gun in her direction and fired.

The bullet nicked her side but didn't stop her from darting away. She ran into the murky dust, zigzagging as the boulder guard fired again and again.

She prayed he didn't hit Lance on his way down the hillside. Instead of climbing, she continued downward, a direction the guard wouldn't expect her to go—toward the cave entrance where she had to see for herself whether the landslide had accomplished its mission. She wasn't sure how far out of the cave the SUV and truck had made it before tons of rocks had crashed down. Even if it hadn't blocked the cave entirely, she hoped the large rocks and boulders would provide enough obstacles it would take Khaled's men a long time to clear a path for them to depart.

Hopefully, enough time for her and Lance to get away and figure out how to notify the Israeli government of the missile stockpile so close to the border.

Besides needing to see the damage for herself, she also had to know if Khaled had lived through the blast and subsequent landslide. The man could not be allowed to continue his reign of terror. Mika owed it to her father and the families of her teammates to make sure Khaled never issued another kill order against innocent family members.

Shouts echoed off the hillside. Shadowy forms moved in the murk ahead.

Mika slowed and ducked low, inching forward as the dust settled.

She crouched, drawing the only weapon she had left on her…the knife sheathed against her thigh.

More shapes emerged from the cloud as the debris and dust slowly settled.

Large rocks and boulders littered the ground, making it difficult to walk without running into them. Many were too large for the truck or SUV to drive over.

Their plan had worked. If not permanently, at

least long enough to slow the terrorists down. They wouldn't be able to move the missiles out of the cave anytime soon.

Now, all Mika needed to do was make sure Khaled was eliminated. Once that was done, she and Lance could leave, get back to the motorcycles and drive until they reached the original extraction point, or found a cellphone tower to get a call through to her unit or his.

She found the boulder and knelt close, her muscles bunched, ready for fight or flight. As the dust dissipated more, she could make out the shape of the SUV in front of her. The vehicle's roof was dented, a huge rock having crashed into it from above. The shattered windshield and battered hood showed the pummeling it had taken in the landslide. Still, it hadn't been completely crushed. The people inside would have survived. Meaning Khaled was still a threat that needed to be neutralized.

Behind the SUV, the cargo truck was half-buried in the rocks, boulders and gravel that had fallen from the bluff. The cave entrance was blocked, and the truckload of missiles wouldn't be going anywhere.

Keeping still, she studied the people moving about, searching for the silvery-white-haired charismatic Hamas leader. Every one of them looked the same, covered in a layer of dust; she couldn't single out the man with the white hair.

About the time she thought it was hopeless,

several of the men gathered around one. He spoke in clear, crisp tones, giving orders.

That had to be Khaled. All she had to do was get close enough. Her hand-to-hand combat skills made up for her smaller size. She'd taken down men who weighed twice as much as her. Cunning and leverage were her tools.

She wanted to call out to Lance, but she didn't dare even whisper when she was surrounded by the enemy. Before long, the cloud would completely dissipate, the sun would rise, and she'd be exposed. She had to make her move soon or be captured without accomplishing their original goal.

She accepted the fact she'd eventually be captured. She doubted she could get away after attacking Khaled. They would likely torture her and drag her dead body in front of video cameras for the world to get the warning to stay out of Palestine and not interfere with Hamas.

She'd die happy to have saved her father's life and the lives of the families of her brothers in arms. One life sacrificed for so many others.

Khaled left the group and picked his way through the rubble, heading toward the boulder, close to where Mika lay in wait.

All she needed was for him to take a few more steps and he'd be past her. She could rise behind him, wrap her arm around his neck and slice through his carotid artery. He'd fall before he could shout for help. She played the scenario repeatedly in her head as her target neared.

When he was only three feet from her position, someone called out from the group moving rocks away from the SUV.

Khaled turned, took one step forward and stopped.

The dust had cleared enough. Mika could see the whites of his eyes shining through the layer of dust coating his face. He took a step.

She had to act fast or miss her chance. He wasn't in front of her, as he had been in her scenario. She was forced to attack from the side. No matter, she'd make it work.

Mika threw herself at the Hamas leader.

He must have caught her movement in his peripheral vision. He stepped back as she reached him.

Committed now, she couldn't go back, fade into the shadow or change her mind.

He swung a fist at her face.

She ducked and rammed her shoulder into his gut, knocking him backward.

He staggered.

Before he could straighten, Mika grabbed his arm, twisted beneath it and brought it up between his shoulders.

A shout rose from the men shifting rocks. They

ran toward her, bring their weapons up and pointing them at her.

With Khaled as her shield, she backed away from the men, calling out in Arabic. "Shoot, and you kill your leader."

With one hand holding Khaled's arm pinned behind his back, she raised the one with the knife to his throat. "Move and he dies."

If she wanted any chance of getting away alive, she had to put enough distance between her and Khaled's men to give her a running start. Under the cover of night, she might make it to the motorcycles before they caught up with her.

The fact she hadn't heard from Lance made her heart squeeze tightly in her chest. He'd had to detonate the explosives before he was ready. Mika prayed he hadn't gotten caught in the landslide. She hoped the only reason he wasn't communicating was that his radio had been damaged. He could be working his way around the hillside now and be there as backup when she made her break for freedom.

Khaled twisted in her grip.

She tightened her hold on the arm she had pinned behind his back, pushing it up higher.

He leaned up on his toes to lessen the pain. "You will die," he said, his tone menacing.

Mika pushed his arm higher, refusing to engage with the murdering bastard.

"Shoot the infidel," he shouted to his men.

They raised their weapons, aiming at Mika and Khaled.

"Shoot!" Khaled demanded. "I sacrifice my life to Allah and Islam."

Still, they hesitated, weapons still pointed in their leader's direction.

If they fired on Khaled, the bullets would go through him and into her.

"Do not allow her to escape. These weapons must reach Israel to destroy those who have stolen the Holy Land from Allah's people. Death to the infidels!"

Khaled's men raised their arms and shouted, "Death to the infidels!"

All the while Khaled spoke, Mika edged backward, dragging him with her, one step at a time, carefully stepping over the debris from the landslide. She maintained a tight hold on his arm while pressing the flat edge of her wickedly sharp knife to the man's throat.

She wasn't ready to give up. As long a Khaled's men continued to hesitate over the order to shoot him and her, she would push forward.

Come on, Lance. Live!

She promised herself that if she survived, she would make that trip to Texas, visit her mother's hometown and take Lance up on his offer to take her fishing.

She'd nearly passed the corner of the giant boulder. Just a little further, and she might accomplish her mission and escape to see another day.

"Shoot!" Khaled commanded.

The sound of gunfire echoed off the hillside, making it seem as if there were several guns firing at once.

Mika's heart leaped, and joy blossomed in her heart and soul.

Lance! Thank the Lord.

He was alive and firing at Khaled's men.

Two of the gunmen dropped where they stood. The others ran for cover behind the SUV.

Mika took that opportunity to duck around the boulder with her hostage.

Moving too fast, she didn't see the rock until she stumbled over it. To keep from falling, she loosened her grip on Khaled's arm and lowered the knife.

Khaled slammed his elbow backward, catching her in the face.

Mika fell back, landing on her ass.

Khaled stood over her, pulled a handgun from beneath his jacket and aimed it at her heart. "You will pay for what you have done with your life, and we will show all of Islam what happens to infidels."

"Not if I can help it," Mika muttered. She brought her booted foot back and kicked Khaled in the knee so hard, she could hear the cartilage pop.

Khaled's leg buckled. He fired off a round, his aim

swinging wide as he teetered and attempted to right himself.

Mika kicked him in the other knee.

Khaled fell backward, landing hard, his head striking a rock.

He lay still, his eyes closed.

Mika scrambled to her feet. She might only have seconds to run, but she wouldn't leave unless she was one-hundred percent certain the Hamas leader was dead.

She leaned over the man and pressed her fingers to the base of his throat, feeling for a pulse.

For a moment, she didn't detect one. Shifting her fingers a little to the right, she held her breath, counting the nanoseconds passing as she verified Khaled's status.

The faint thumping of blood beneath the surface of the skin gave Mika her answer. She reached for her knife, lying on the ground two feet away, the blade shining in the starlight.

As she raised it to finish the job, Khaled's eyes flashed open, and he caught Mika's wrist in an iron grip.

She twisted her arm, fighting to free herself.

Khaled bucked beneath her, rolled her onto her back and straddled her hips. He released her wrist and wrapped his hands around her throat.

No matter how hard she fought, she could not

break free of his chokehold. She scratched at his face, kicked up her knees, but nothing helped.

The longer he applied pressure to her throat, the less oxygen made it to her brain.

The stars above her faded into a gray haze as she slipped deeper into unconsciousness. Her thoughts drifted to Lance and their night of passion beneath those very stars. She wished she'd had more time with the man. If only they'd met sooner. If only...

Khaled jerked upward and off her, releasing his hold on her neck.

The rush of air into her lungs sent much-needed oxygen to her starving brain. Seconds later, the fog cleared, and she sat up.

Khaled lay on the ground, his throat cut, his eyes staring blankly up at the stars fading from the sky as the pre-dawn light crept up the eastern horizon.

Lance reached down with his free hand and pulled her to her feet and into his chest. "You all right?"

She nodded, leaning against him long enough for her legs to steady.

Men rushed around the corner of the boulder.

Lance lowered his rifle and fired, dropping the first two.

The men behind him fell back behind the boulder.

"Run," Lance commanded.

"Not without you," she said.

"I've got your back; you need to get to the motorcycles. I'll be right behind you." He gave her a gentle shove. "Go."

Another man rounded the boulder and opened fire.

Lance shoved Mika behind him and returned fire.

The man ducked back around the boulder.

"Go!" Lance urged.

Mika didn't want to leave him. She reasoned that if she got to the motorcycles, she could swing back and pick him up. With her driving, he could continue to cover their backs.

With that plan in mind, she ran as fast as she could down the road leading away from the hill.

Her lungs burned, and her muscles screamed. She didn't slow until she arrived at the ravine.

She lifted the motorcycle onto its wheels, slung her leg over the seat and started the engine. A moment later, she popped up out of the ravine, spun around and sped back to the hill and Lance.

She prayed she wasn't too late.

CHAPTER 13

Lance held off the Hamas fighters, knowing it was only a matter of time before they found another way around the boulder and cut him off from any chance of escape.

The sound of a motorcycle engine made hope flare. Mika had made it to the ravine. She would make it out alive.

When the engine noise grew louder, Lance frowned. He dared to look over his shoulder for a second only to see Mika bent low over the body of the bike, racing straight for him as the gray light of dawn edged upward on the horizon.

He turned too late to see one of the gunmen raising his weapon, aiming straight at Lance.

He dove to the left as a bullet slammed into his calf. It stung, but the adrenaline pulsing through his system kept him upright and firing back.

He dropped the man and fired at the next one who leaped out to take his place.

That one fired once and ducked back behind the boulder.

Mika spun around him and stopped long enough for him to straddle the seat and hold on. He turned, aiming his rifle behind them.

Mika goosed the throttle and sent them speeding away from the hill filled with missiles and Hamas fighters.

The gunmen ran out from behind the boulder, firing everything they had at Lance and Mika. By then, they were far enough away that the bullets went wide or fell short.

Lance hugged Mika around her middle, amazed at her bravery and thankful she hadn't given up on him. He glanced back once more at the hill that wouldn't release its contents anytime soon.

His stomach roiled. Just when he thought they were home free, he saw the banged-up SUV pull around the boulder, bump across debris and clear the rubble.

"We have company," he shouted. However, Lance wasn't too worried. With a ruined tire, the SUV wouldn't catch them.

At that moment, the motorcycle engine coughed, sputtered and died.

They rolled to a stop in the middle of the road with nothing to get behind for cover and protection.

Lance slid off the back of the bike. As soon as his feet touched the ground, his leg gave out, the injury making itself known. He dropped to his knees.

"Lay the bike down and get behind it," he said.

Mika dropped the motorcycle onto its side and lay on her belly behind it. "You're injured. Give me the rifle."

He didn't argue, handing the rifle over to her. She was every bit as good a warrior as he was. Maybe better. Pulling his handgun from the holster at his hip, he held it out in front of him and waited for the SUV to get close enough his bullets might count.

Mika started firing as soon as the vehicle came in range. Nothing she did slowed it.

"Be ready to move," Lance said.

Mika held the rifle steady, emptying the magazine of all the bullets. Steam rose from the front of the vehicle.

The SUV kept coming.

A familiar sound caught Lance's attention. The thumping rhythm of rotor blades whipping the air came from behind them.

As he handed another magazine to Mika, Lance glanced over his shoulder. His heart slammed against his ribs at the sight of a Black Hawk helicopter flying low over the horizon, sweeping in with the fiery blaze of dawn.

He wanted to shout and cheer, but they weren't safe yet. Not with the SUV still advancing.

A whoop rose from the woman beside him as she renewed her attack on the SUV lumbering toward them.

She didn't have to do much. As soon as the crew of the Black Hawk came close enough to evaluate the situation, Mika spoke, her voice coming through his headset, more as static than words. More static followed.

Mika touched his arm. "Stay down," she said and ducked her head.

The Black Hawk swooped low and rained .50 caliber bullets on the SUV. It swerved, sped up and ran off the road, crashing into the ditch. No one made it out.

The Black Hawk circled and landed ten yards from Lance and Mika. Seven men leaped out and ran toward them.

Lance had never been so happy to see his team as he was at that moment. He tried to stand, but Mika put a hand on his shoulder. "Let them help you."

Rucker was first to reach him. He slung one of Lance's arms over his shoulder. "We thought we'd never find you. It wasn't until you sent up that smoke signal that we had a clue as to where you and Mika had disappeared."

Tank looped his other arm over his shoulder. "Catch a bullet?"

"I took one for the team," Lance said.

"You didn't take one for this team," Mac said.

"Maybe for your adopted team of one female IDF soldier."

"I'd join that team," Blade grinned. "She's a lot better to look at than this bunch of boneheads."

"Hey," Dash puffed out his chest. "Speak for yourself. My girl says I'm the sexiest man alive."

Bull snorted. "Sunny Daye must be blinded by the spotlights. I sure don't see it."

Lance grinned at the banter his teammates threw around. They all liked to joke, but when the shit got real, they were there.

Rucker and Tank loaded him onto the helicopter, forcing him to lie on the floor while Mika got a spot on the bench seat.

Lance wanted to sit beside her and hold her hand as he'd done on their flight into West Bank.

Tank had other ideas. He busied himself applying first aid to the bullet wound on Lance's calf. He didn't care. He had a good view of the amazing woman he'd come to respect over the past few days. Not only did he respect her, he'd swear he was well on his way to falling in love with her

He hoped to get her alone as soon as they landed back in Jerusalem. He'd ask to be extended in Israel so that he could debrief the IDF on what they'd found stashed in a cave in the West Bank. Surely, they'd want a detailed account of everything. That could take days, right?

Whatever he had to do, he would do it, just to get

to spend more time with Mika Blue, warrior princess and phenomenal lover. He had a lot he wanted to say to her, but he needed time for her to come to the same conclusion he'd arrived at when he'd seen Khaled Aziz choking the life out of her.

Lance wanted Mika in his life. Permanently. If it meant leaving Delta Force and moving to Israel, he'd do it. She was worth it. He crossed his arms behind his head and grinned.

"Is that morphine working for you already?" Tank asked.

Lance frowned. He could still feel the pain in his leg. "No, why?"

"You have a stupid grin on your face." Tank laughed. "By the way, I haven't given you any morphine, so it isn't the painkiller putting that look on your face. So, what did?"

"I'm thinking about the fishing I'm going to do when I get home."

"Yeah, right." Tank shook his head. "No amount of fishing puts that kind of grin on a man's face." He tipped his head toward Mika. "That's the kind of grin a woman can make happen. You want to tell us what's going on?"

Lance shook his head, his grin broadening. "Nope."

. . .

LANCE TOLD Rucker and the Black Hawk pilot about the stash of missiles. The pilot relayed the coordinates to the Israeli Defense Force who promised to destroy them as soon as possible.

Mika worried about Lance's wound as they crossed the border, heading for Jerusalem. He'd lost some blood and his face was a little pale. She didn't have to worry long, though.

After his teammate cleaned and dressed the wound, Lance leaned back with a huge grin on his face.

Next, the medic dressed the wound on Mika's side. It was nothing more than a flesh wound, nothing that would put her out of commission for any length of time.

It was the smile on Lance's face that had her thinking. Her lips quirked at his obvious happiness. And why wouldn't he be happy? They were alive. Khaled was dead, and they were on their way back to the base where they could shower, eat and sleep for a couple of days. They'd accomplished the mission, discovered a stockpile of missiles and lived to tell about it.

The fact that they'd made love beneath the starlight didn't have to come up in any of the briefings. That was something between Lance and Mika. No one else. She hoped he didn't have to head back to the States right away. She wanted to spend some time with him so he could make good on his promise to make love to her in a proper bed.

She found herself grinning as broadly as Lance by the time they landed. Never had she returned from a mission with such a sense of satisfaction. She suspected it had a lot more to do with making love in the starlight than taking a deadly terrorist out of commission and uncovering a secret stash of missiles.

Even more so, the grin had a lot to do with the anticipation of things to come. Soon, she hoped.

EPILOGUE

"When did you say your teammates would arrive?" Mika asked from inside the cabin bathroom.

"About an hour," Lance responded. He'd spent the past two hours rigging fishing poles for Mika and her father, who'd arrived the night before at the tiny airport in Temple, Texas.

The poles were gifts he'd taken the time and effort to select especially for this vacation Mika had arranged following the highly successful conclusion of the mission to free the world of one particularly nasty terrorist.

Lance had performed additional temporary duty or TDY, remaining in Jerusalem for three weeks following that mission to debrief the IDF and members of the Israeli government officials on the stash he and Mika had found and foiled.

The IDF leaders took the information and ran

with it, unwilling to wait for the government decision-makers to drag their feet and allow sufficient time for Hamas to dig the missiles out of the hill and shuffle them to an unknown location.

For the three weeks he spent in Jerusalem, he slept every night with Mika. If not in his hotel, then it was in her barracks. She sneaked him in. They both liked the additional adrenaline inspired by the potential of getting caught.

They'd learned that they were sexually compatible on a rocky hillside as well as in a soft bed, on a table, countertop, sofa, shower and bathtub.

Whenever they had a spare minute, they found a quiet place where no one could watch them kiss, run their hands over each other's bodies and occasionally make love against the wall inside a closet.

He'd left at the end of the three weeks, wondering how they'd make things work on a more permanent basis.

The day after he'd returned to Texas, while standing at the window of his apartment, he'd thought about Mika and how much he already missed her. At that moment, a text had pinged on his cellphone.

He'd smiled to see it was Mika.

Mika: Booked a flight to Temple. Arriving in a week. Bringing my father. Hoping you can take us fishing.

Lance: You bet. I know just the place. Miss you already.

Mika: I missed you before you left. Long-distance relationships suck.

He'd hustled to book the cabin by the lake. The cabin was two-bedroom and came with a couple of kayaks, paddleboards and a grill.

He'd worked with Rucker and Dash to come up with an excursion that would take Mika's father out of the cabin for a couple of hours the first day so that Lance and Mika could have some time alone. They'd spent the entire time naked in bed, making love.

Lance taught Mika's father how to kayak and paddleboard on the lake, sending him off for an hour at a time while he sneaked back into the cabin for time alone with Mika.

For their last day in the cabin, they'd planned a cookout, inviting all of Lance's team and his teammates' significant others. Most had decided to stop at the Salty Dog Saloon for a drink before arriving at the cabin. Rucker came by to collect Mr. Blum so that he could enjoy the comradery of military guys sharing war stories over a mug of beer.

After finishing with the fishing poles, Lance stood, stretched and turned toward the bathroom where Mika was getting ready. "What do I need to do to get ready?"

She appeared in the doorway, wearing nothing but a smile. "I'd say you're a bit overdressed for one."

He grinned and pulled her into his arms. "I can fix that."

"You better hurry. I think Dash said he'd be here early to help get the grill going." She tugged his shirt out of the waistband of his jeans.

He chuckled. "Bossy much?"

"Only when I want something."

He unbuttoned his jeans and lowered the zipper. "And what is it you want?"

She slid her hands over his bare ass and squeezed gently. "You." When she tried to help him push his pants over his hips, she bumped into a hard, square object in his pocket. "What do you have there? A whole box of condoms?"

He laughed out loud and shrugged the rest of the way out of his clothes. Before he dropped his jeans in a chair, he fished the box out of the pocket and spoke in a rush. "I meant to do this in front of everyone, but that might be a bad idea, considering I have no idea what your answer will be. You might think it's too soon, but I've been thinking about this since that night in the West Bank when we made love beneath the stars."

Mika laughed. "Are you nervous? I don't think I've ever heard you talk this fast and make so little sense."

"Yes, I'm nervous. This could be a big deal." He frowned, turning the box in his hand. "Well, it is a big deal to me, and somehow, I don't think I should be doing this…naked."

Mika shook her head. "I have no idea what you're talking about."

Lance took a deep breath and dropped to one knee. "Mikayla Blum, I'm terribly, madly, deeply in love with you."

She gasped and covered her mouth with her hand. Her eyes grew large and full of tears. "You love me?"

"Of course, I do. I wouldn't string a fishing pole for just anyone." He drew in another steadying breath and continued. "I know we live in two different countries and have careers that will mean spending most of our time apart, but I think we can make it work. I have another five years until I retire. I'm willing to do whatever we have to in order for us to be together when we can. Then when I retire, I'll follow you, get a job and live wherever you want. Anywhere, as long as I get to be with you." He looked up into her eyes. "Mika, will you marry me?"

Tears trickled from the corners of her eyes, making trails through her freshly applied makeup. "Are you sure?"

He cocked an eyebrow. "As sure as I can be, kneeling on a cool floor, naked as the day I was born and loving you so much, I think my heart might explode. Yes. I'm positive."

Holding his breath, he waited for her answer.

She cupped his cheek in her palm and bent to press her lips to his. She drew him to his feet. "Yes. I would be honored to become your wife."

Lance pulled a beautiful diamond solitaire out of the box and slid it onto her finger.

She smiled down at the ring, and then up into his eyes. "And just so you know, lately, I've considered leaving the military."

He frowned. "Not because of me, I hope."

She shook her head. "Yes and no. I love you and want to be your wife. I don't want to wait five years to be together."

"I could quit the Army and follow you," he offered.

"I want you and a family of our own. I don't want to be pregnant on a battlefield. And I want to be there for our babies."

Lance's heart swelled so tightly he was sure he was having a heart attack. "Babies?"

She nodded. "As long as you do."

He swept her up into his arms. "Hell, yes! Could we start working on them now?"

She laughed and kissed him. "I was hoping we could. I'm not getting any younger, and I want at least half a dozen."

"Sweet Jesus. I think we can manage that." He laid her out on the bed and dropped down beside her. "Maybe we should tell the others the party is off. We have work to do." He kissed her lips and every part of her body.

This wonderful woman was going to be his wife. Together, they'd make a family.

As he drove into her, he laughed and said, "We're going to need more fishing poles."

BREAKING PROMISES

BROTHERHOOD PROTECTORS
COLORADO BOOK #1

New York Times & USA Today
Bestselling Author

ELLE JAMES

CHAPTER 1

"KETCH AND GONZO, IN POSITION." Xavier Gonzalez said into the radio. "Go!"

Asher "Smoke" Gray passed his two Delta Force teammates and leaped forward from one building to the next, the steady sound of rocket fire leading him toward his target. His Israeli Special Forces counterpart, David Nassar, kept pace with him, three steps behind. The two highly trained operators had chosen to take point as the most skilled snipers. Their mission was to take out the Hamas terrorists orchestrating the rocket bombardment of Israel that had gone on for the past three nights as retribution for the confiscation of a cargo ship carrying medical supplies destined for the Gaza Strip.

Israeli intelligence had received information that the ship had in fact contained medical supplies. However, buried beneath the medical supplies had been a massive shipment of arms to resupply Hamas on the Strip. The Israeli Navy intercepted the ship and took it into their base at the Port of Haifa.

As Smoke moved along the street, he clung to the shadows, careful not to expose himself to streetlights or potential sentries guarding the rocket launcher location. Once Smoke and Nassar were in position, Gonzo and Master Sergeant Karl Ketchum would follow. Voodoo, Rome, Ice and five men from the Israeli Special Forces, or Sayeret, had fanned out, moving forward on parallel streets, closing in on the target. If needed, they would provide a distraction to allow Smoke and Nassar to get close enough to take out their targets. Once they eliminated the men launching the rockets, they could work on disabling the rocket launcher. Blowing up the launcher wasn't an option, not when Hamas had parked it in the middle of a populated area. Destroying the launcher might ignite the remaining rockets and devastate the area. The civilian collateral damage wouldn't go unnoticed. Not with Hamas's news and social media propaganda machine.

Smoke peeked around the corner of a building toward an open area that appeared to have been a park. A truck with a hydraulic lift on the back stood in the park's center.

The launcher was nearly empty with only two rockets remaining. An additional stack of another six rockets stood several yards from the truck. Intel estimated Hamas had a stash of thousands of rockets to refill the battery and continue its onslaught. Destroying the launcher was imperative.

A group of men, armed with AK-47s, surrounded the truck and the launcher. Some guarded the perimeter. Others stared at the launcher.

With a quick, thorough assessment of the people standing in the park, Smoke raised his rifle and stared through his digital night vision scope, sighted in on the man wearing loose, black trousers and a black tunic, sporting an equally black turban on his head. He appeared to be the one in charge. The terrorist stood with his shoulders back, his head held high. A man approached him, carrying a radio on his back. He spoke briefly, nodded and turned away.

Smoke studied the leader who had a short, dark beard, high cheekbones, heavy eyebrows and a prominent nose. He matched the image of the Hamas leader they had been briefed on prior to executing this mission. He had the nose, the eyebrows and the high cheekbones, but he didn't have the scar from the corner of his right eye to the edge of his mouth, and his beard was shorter and darker. He waved his hand, and another rocket shot into the air with a fiery blast, shaking the ground around them. Only one rocket remained in the battery of empty shells.

Out of the corner of his eye, he saw Nassar moving into his position on the opposite side of the street, using the corner of another building as cover.

Smoke waited until the other sniper had his rifle braced against his shoulder.

"I have the primary target in my sights." Smoke said softly into his mic, his finger resting lightly on the trigger.

"In position," Nassar said. "Secondary target acquired."

"Let's get this party started," Gonzo said. "Make it quick. We don't want to be surprised by incoming from the rear."

Smoke focused on his bogey. "Ready?" he whispered into his mic.

"Ready," Nassar responded.

"Ready," Ketch echoed.

"On three," Smoke said. "One…Two…Three." He held his breath and caressed the trigger. The silencer at the end of his barrel muffled the sound of the bullet leaving the rifle.

The leader's eyes widened. He stood still for a moment, and then fell to his knees and crashed to the ground. Another man near the launcher dropped at the same time.

At first, the other men around the park didn't realize what was happening, giving Smoke and Nassar a chance to pick off two more each. By that time, shouts sounded, and the perimeter guards fired their AK-47s indiscriminately at the dark streets and alleys surrounding them.

The other Deltas and Israelis joined in the fight.

One of the Hamas men dropped to his belly, rolled behind the stack of rockets and fired toward the corners where Smoke and Nassar had established their positions.

Smoke couldn't return fire for fear of hitting the rockets and setting off a firestorm of explosions.

Instead, he had to withdraw behind the corner enough to protect himself and focus his attention on other men in less precarious and more exposed positions.

A moment later, a small dark object sailed through the air, landing in front of Nassar's face where he lay prone. He scrambled to his feet and kicked the object like a professional soccer player, aiming for a mid-field goal.

"Take cover!" he yelled and dove behind the building.

Smoke flung himself back behind the building, hoping the other joint team members did the same.

A blast sounded.

Smoke scrambled to his feet and ran, covering his ears.

A moment later, a deafening explosion ripped through the sky, slamming through the surrounding structures. The force of the blast flung Smoke forward. He landed hard on his belly as debris erupted from buildings, raining down on him. He covered his head and the back of his neck with his arms and tucked his face into his shirt. The wall of the business beside him crumbled and toppled down, the bulk of which narrowly missed crushing him. Dust filled the air like a dense fog, making it impossible to see more than a foot in front of his face.

As soon as he could, Smoke lurched to his feet, his ears ringing and his lungs choking on the fine particles of dust filling the air. He pulled a large dark scrap of cloth from one of his cargo pockets and wrapped it around his face and neck, pulling it up over his mouth and nose to prevent the dust from entering his lungs. He tapped the headset on his helmet. "Deltas?"

A moment passed. Then another.

Silence.

His heart hammering against his ribs, Smoke turned in the eerie haze. Buildings around him were so damaged by the blast their walls were ruptured or gone. The street filled with rubble made it difficult to know what was street and what was building. Smoke didn't know where to begin looking for his teammates.

A man appeared out of the mist, his body covered in a layer of gray, fine powder, a rifle in his hands.

Smoke raised his weapon, pointing at the man's chest. "Halt, who goes there?"

The man coughed. "Nassar," he choked out.

Smoke lowered his rifle and touched a finger to the side of his helmet. "Do you have coms?"

Nassar shook his head.

"We need to move to our extraction point," Smoke said through the cloth over his face.

"The others?" Nassar coughed and covered his mouth with the front of his shirt as he dragged in a shaky breath.

"The others will move toward the extraction point. We'll regroup there." And count heads. If anyone was missing, Smoke would be back to find him.

Nassar nodded and started down the middle of the street, his rifle held ready to fire.

Smoke followed, turning around every so often to check his six. As he passed another crumbled building, the pile of rubble near his feet stirred.

Smoke jumped back, aiming his weapon at the debris.

A figure emerged and staggered to his feet. He carried a dirty rifle and wore a helmet covered in the thick powder caused by the destruction.

Smoke leaned toward him. "Ketch?"

"Yeah," the man responded and hacked up half his lung. "Where's Gonzo?"

A couple of yards away, what had appeared to be debris from a fallen wall, rolled over. "Here," Gonzo called out, raising a hand as if at roll call in school. "Did you get the number of the truck that hit me?"

Smoke hurried over to him, extended a hand and hesitated. "Injuries?"

"My ears are ringing so loud I can't think, and my

head hurts like a mother fuc—" He curled into a ball and coughed hard. One hand clutched at his belly, the other at his head, and he moaned.

His own head aching from the force of the concussion, Smoke understood. "We need to get moving before reinforcements pour in and cut us off from our extraction point."

Gonzo gripped Smoke's hand.

As Smoke braced himself, the other man pulled himself to his feet, standing a few inches shorter than Smoke. He swayed for a second, then squared his shoulders, a frown pulling his brow low. "Hear anything from the others?"

Smoke tapped the side of his helmet and shook his head. "My comms are out."

"Mine, too," Ketch said.

"Same," Gonzo added. "Hopefully, the others are on their way."

They moved quickly through the streets, back to the water where the combat rubber raiding rafts had been stashed between the myriad of fishing boats in the Port of Gaza, waiting to take them out under cover of darkness as they arrived. They could have beached the Zodiac watercraft on the long stretch of beach, but they'd determined it would be easier to hide among the fishing and pleasure boats moored near the port. And it was easier to find cover and concealment there than on an empty beach in the open.

Smoke took the lead, his hearing still impacted but slowly improving. They had a lot of ground to cover in a short amount of time.

Sirens sounded, moving toward them.

Smoke ducked into a dark alley. Gonzo, Ketch and Nassar followed.

An ambulance raced past them, heading for ground zero of the rocket explosion.

"I only heard the grenade and then one rocket go off. From what I could see, there was a stack of six more rockets lying on the ground," he said.

"We're lucky they didn't all explode," Gonzo said.

"We wouldn't be walking here if they had," Ketch said, his jaw set in a tight line.

"Hopefully, the one rocket destroyed the launcher, so they can't load the remaining six," Smoke said.

After the ambulance passed, Gonzo took a step toward the street.

Smoke snagged his arm and pulled him back.

A truck raced past moments later, filled with heavily armed Hamas soldiers, hurrying to get to the site of the explosion.

"Thanks," Gonzo said.

Smoke hoped all the team had gotten out. The terrorists wouldn't go easy on any opposing forces found deep inside enemy territory.

They continued through the streets, avoiding any other humans at all costs. They weren't supposed to be behind the enemy lines. And the US Delta Force operatives weren't supposed to get involved with the ongoing war between the Palestinians and the Israelis.

Then why the hell was Delta Force in Gaza? And why were they helping the Israeli Defense Force Sayerets curb the delivery of rockets that were lobbed into villages of innocent Israeli civilians? The politicians in Washington must have decided to provide assistance as a show of benevolence and support of the Israeli government. The Deltas were mere pawns in their global political wargames.

Smoke had a lot of respect for the men and women of the Sayerets, having been on another mission recently into the West Bank. They were a highly-trained unit of fierce fighters, every bit as good as what the US had to offer. He was proud to work alongside them. The death and destruction Hamas served up daily needed to stop. Until it did, there would be no negotiations between the two sides.

Ahead, Smoke caught glimpses of the starlight reflecting off the water of the Mediterranean Sea. His pulse quickened along with his footsteps. Movement in his peripheral vision made him look to his right as he crossed a street.

A dark figure, carrying a heavy load on his back, moved from shadow to shadow, heading toward the sea on a street parallel to the one on which Smoke currently stood.

Smoke raised his fist, indicating the others should halt. He ran down the cross street and slipped up behind the man, carrying his load.

The burden he carried moaned and moved an arm.

He wasn't dead. But, depending on his injuries, he could go south quickly.

When Smoke was within ten feet of the man, he called out softly, "Marco," he challenged.

"Polo," the man responded.

Though the face was completely covered in dust, relief flooded Smoke as he recognized the voice. "Voodoo," he said. "Who's this?"

"Rome," he answered, his tone terse. "The blast knocked him backward. He hit the ground hard. He also caught some shrapnel. It's embedded in his left shin."

Moving back into the shadows, Smoke took one of Rome's arms and moved in closer. "I'll take him."

Voodoo, legally known as Beau Guidry, shook his head. "I've got him."

"Dude, you brought him far enough." Smoke handing his weapon to Gonzo. "Let me take over."

Ketch and Gonzo lifted Rome off Voodoo's shoulder and settled him onto Smoke, piggy-back style.

"Hold on, buddy. We'll get you back." With his arms looped around Rome's legs, Smoke took off, heading for the port.

Ketch and Gonzo took point. Voodoo and Nassar had Smoke's six. They moved quickly. Smoke hoped that the other members of their team would be waiting at the dock, already in the boats, ready to punch out.

Ahead, Ketch raised his fist.

Smoke stopped, clinging to the shadow of a building. Rome's breath on the back of his neck reassured him that the man was still alive.

Ketch gave the signal to follow him, and they continued through the streets.

A block short of the port, they stopped in an alley between buildings.

"I'm going forward," Ketch said. "I'll flash a red light once if the boats are compromised. Twice for all clear." The man slipped away, moving quickly and silently past the buildings and across the road in front of the rudimentary Port of Gaza.

Voodoo and Nassar positioned themselves several yards to their rear, guarding their rear. Gonzo left Smoke's rifle leaning against the side of the building next to Smoke and Rome. He moved to the end of the block, knelt at the forward edge of the building there and covered for Ketch while he made his way to the boats.

Smoke leaned his back, with Rome, against a building and waited for what seemed like forever. "Hanging in there, Rome?" he asked.

Rome grunted.

"So, you're still with us, huh?" Smoke nodded. "Don't worry. We'll get you back to Jerusalem before you know it."

"Sure," Rome said, his voice weak.

"You know," Smoke said. "No man left behind."

"Damn right," Rome whispered.

A moment later, a pinpoint of red light flashed once amid the fishing boats tied to the pier.

Smoke tensed and leaned forward, taking all of Rome's weight. He held his breath, praying for the second flash for all clear.

After the longest second of his life, the red light flashed a second time.

Smoke released the breath he'd been holding and leaned forward, taking all of Rome's weight he'd been resting against the wall. "That's our cue. Let's blow this joint."

He waved to Voodoo and Nassar. When they were within a couple of yards of him, he turned toward the sea, quickly closing the distance between him and Gonzo.

Gonzo checked right and left then stepped out into the open. "Go," he said.

Smoke moved as quickly as he could with the man on his back across the open space, the street and onto the pier.

Once again, his team surrounded him, moving quickly. As they approached the location where they'd tucked the boats between a row of fishing boats, Ketch straightened from a kneeling position, and men rose from where they sat in the rubber crafts. They held out their arms for Rome.

Gonzo and Ketch eased the man off Smoke's back and handed him down into one of the boats. Voodoo and Gonzo dropped over the side of the pier into the same boat.

"Everyone here?" Smoke asked.

Ketch nodded. "All present. Get in. We've pushed our luck so far."

Smoke glanced behind him once more.

The dark silhouettes of men moving their way made his pulse quicken. "Time to bug out."

Ketch swore. "Couldn't wait another five minutes, could they?"

Smoke dove into the boat as the boat drivers fired up the engines. The first boat took off with its load of Sayerets and Deltas.

Ketch remained on the pier a moment longer than Smoke, his weapon trained on the approaching men. As soon as the engine roared to life, Ketch dropped down into the boat. As soon as his feet hit the rubber, the driver whipped the boat around and raced through the maze of fishing boats.

Shouts and shots rang out behind them.

Smoke, Gonzo, Nassar and others fired back as they broke free of the moored boats and headed out into open water.

For a moment, Smoke breathed a sigh of relief.

Then what appeared to be an old military-style PT boat whipped out of the port behind them, men on the front of the rig firing.

The military boat, made for moving swiftly through the water, would catch them before long.

Smoke conserved his ammunition until the larger, faster boat got closer. The Zodiac rubber boats bounced in the swells.

His heart pounding, Smoke held onto the boat and his weapon as the advancing boat closed the distance between them.

Just when Smoke raised his weapon to fire, the rapid staccato of fifty-caliber machinegun fire rent the air overhead.

Despite the rain of bullets, the trailing vessel didn't slow until a flash of light and an explosion ripped through the hull. The boat rocked to a stop, fire rising from the deck.

Without slowing, the Zodiacs continued out to sea a little further. The Chinook helicopter above made a wide circle, then lowered to the water, immersing its belly enough to lower the ramp. The first rubber boat sped up and drove up the ramp and into the chopper. Without hesitating, Smoke's boat driver followed, picking up speed. When the rubber hit the ramp, they slid up into the fuselage. Men leaped over the sides, grabbed the sides of the rubber raft and hauled it the rest of the way into the bird. The ramp rose as the helicopter lifted out of the water and into the sky.

They weren't safe until they were well beyond the range of heat-seeking missiles. The chopper rose high into the sky and headed north toward Tel Aviv. When they were far enough away, Smoke dared to breathe normally.

The team medic had Rome hooked up to an IV and had dressed his wound, stabilizing the man until they reached a higher level of medical care.

Smoke leaned back on the bench, his head pounding, his hearing barely returned to normal.

"Well, that didn't go quite as planned," Gonzo said.

Several helmets flew across the interior of the helicopter at Gonzo, and some of the men chuckled, breaking the tension.

No, the operation hadn't gone as planned, but if Smoke had learned anything in his thirteen years in the military…plans were useless, but planning was necessary. What was done was done. They'd accomplished their mission. The rocket launcher had been destroyed.

Along with half a city block because a Hamas terrorist had thought it was a good idea to lob a grenade.

The mission debrief and after-action report would be interesting, to say the least. They might all be reassigned after what had happened.

ABOUT THE AUTHOR

ELLE JAMES also writing as MYLA JACKSON is a *New York Times* and *USA Today* Bestselling author of books including cowboys, intrigues and paranormal adventures that keep her readers on the edges of their seats. When she's not at her computer, she's traveling, snow skiing, boating, or riding her ATV, dreaming up new stories. Learn more about Elle James at www.ellejames.com

Website | Facebook | Twitter | GoodReads |
Newsletter | BookBub | Amazon

Or visit her alter ego Myla Jackson at
mylajackson.com
Website | Facebook | Twitter | Newsletter

Follow Me!
www.ellejames.com
ellejamesauthor@gmail.com

ALSO BY ELLE JAMES

Brotherhood Protectors International

Athens Affair (#1)

Belgian Betrayal (#2)

Croatia Collateral (#3)

Dublin Debacle (#4)

Edinburgh Escape (#5)

Brotherhood Protectors Hawaii

Kalea's Hero (#1)

Leilani's Hero (#2)

Kiana's Hero (#3)

Maliea's Hero (#4)

Emi's Hero (#5)

Sachie's Hero (#6)

Kimo's Hero (#7)

Alana's Hero (#8)

Nala's Hero (#9)

Mika's Hero (#10)

Bayou Brotherhood Protectors

Remy (#1)

Gerard (#2)

Lucas (#3)

Beau (#4)

Rafael (#5)

Valentin (#6)

Landry (#7)

Simon (#8)

Maurice (#9)

Jacques (#10)

Brotherhood Protectors Yellowstone

Saving Kyla (#1)

Saving Chelsea (#2)

Saving Amanda (#3)

Saving Liliana (#4)

Saving Breely (#5)

Saving Savvie (#6)

Saving Jenna (#7)

Saving Peyton (#8)

Saving Londyn (#9)

Brotherhood Protectors Colorado

SEAL Salvation (#1)

Rocky Mountain Rescue (#2)

Ranger Redemption (#3)
Tactical Takeover (#4)
Colorado Conspiracy (#5)
Rocky Mountain Madness (#6)
Free Fall (#7)
Colorado Cold Case (#8)
Fool's Folly (#9)
Colorado Free Rein (#10)
Rocky Mountain Venom (#11)
High Country Hero (#12)

Brotherhood Protectors

Montana SEAL (#1)
Bride Protector SEAL (#2)
Montana D-Force (#3)
Cowboy D-Force (#4)
Montana Ranger (#5)
Montana Dog Soldier (#6)
Montana SEAL Daddy (#7)
Montana Ranger's Wedding Vow (#8)
Montana SEAL Undercover Daddy (#9)
Cape Cod SEAL Rescue (#10)
Montana SEAL Friendly Fire (#11)
Montana SEAL's Mail-Order Bride (#12)

SEAL Justice (#13)

Ranger Creed (#14)

Delta Force Rescue (#15)

Dog Days of Christmas (#16)

Montana Rescue (#17)

Montana Ranger Returns (#18)

Brotherhood Protectors Boxed Set 1

Brotherhood Protectors Boxed Set 2

Brotherhood Protectors Boxed Set 3

Brotherhood Protectors Boxed Set 4

Brotherhood Protectors Boxed Set 5

Brotherhood Protectors Boxed Set 6

Iron Horse Legacy

Soldier's Duty (#1)

Ranger's Baby (#2)

Marine's Promise (#3)

SEAL's Vow (#4)

Warrior's Resolve (#5)

Drake (#6)

Grimm (#7)

Murdock (#8)

Utah (#9)

Judge (#10)

Delta Force Strong

Ivy's Delta (Delta Force 3 Crossover)

Breaking Silence (#1)

Breaking Rules (#2)

Breaking Away (#3)

Breaking Free (#4)

Breaking Hearts (#5)

Breaking Ties (#6)

Breaking Point (#7)

Breaking Dawn (#8)

Breaking Promises (#9)

Hearts & Heroes Series

Wyatt's War (#1)

Mack's Witness (#2)

Ronin's Return (#3)

Sam's Surrender (#4)

Hellfire Series

Hellfire, Texas (#1)

Justice Burning (#2)

Smoldering Desire (#3)

Hellfire in High Heels (#4)

Playing With Fire (#5)

Up in Flames (#6)

Total Meltdown (#7)

Take No Prisoners Series

SEAL's Honor (#1)

SEAL'S Desire (#2)

SEAL's Embrace (#3)

SEAL's Obsession (#4)

SEAL's Proposal (#5)

SEAL's Seduction (#6)

SEAL'S Defiance (#7)

SEAL's Deception (#8)

SEAL's Deliverance (#9)

SEAL's Ultimate Challenge (#10)

Texas Billionaire Club

Tarzan & Janine (#1)

Something To Talk About (#2)

Who's Your Daddy (#3)

Love & War (#4)

Billionaire Online Dating Service

The Billionaire Husband Test (#1)

The Billionaire Cinderella Test (#2)

The Billionaire Bride Test (#3)

The Billionaire Daddy Test (#4)

The Billionaire Matchmaker Test (#5)

The Billionaire Glitch Date (#6)

The Billionaire Perfect Date (#7) coming soon

The Billionaire Replacement Date (#8) coming soon

The Billionaire Wedding Date (#9) coming soon

Cajun Magic Mystery Series

Voodoo on the Bayou (#1)

Voodoo for Two (#2)

Deja Voodoo (#3)

Cajun Magic Mysteries Books 1-3

The Outriders

Homicide at Whiskey Gulch (#1)

Hideout at Whiskey Gulch (#2)

Held Hostage at Whiskey Gulch (#3)

Setup at Whiskey Gulch (#4)

Missing Witness at Whiskey Gulch (#5)

Cowboy Justice at Whiskey Gulch (#6)

Boys Behaving Badly Anthologies

Rogues (#1)

Blue Collar (#2)

Pirates (#3)

Stranded (#4)

First Responder (#5)

Cowboys (#6)

Silver Soldiers (#7)

Secret Identities (#8)

Warrior's Conquest

Enslaved by the Viking Short Story

Conquests

Smokin' Hot Firemen

Protecting the Colton Bride

Protecting the Colton Bride & Colton's Cowboy Code

Heir to Murder

Secret Service Rescue

High Octane Heroes

Haunted

Engaged with the Boss

Cowboy Brigade

An Unexpected Clue

Under Suspicion, With Child

Texas-Size Secrets